Song for an Eagle

By

Catherine M Byrne

Acknowledgements

My thanks to the following people who helped get
this book ready for publication.
Tutor George Gunn and The North Highland College
course for creative writing, my beta readers, Margaret
MacKay, Margaret Wood, Tom Allan, Sheona Campell
and of course, as usual, the members of my writer's
circles.

Song for an Eagle

Prologue

When Beth was five years old, her mother walked out and never returned. The child had a memory of terror, terror of being left alone. She stood by the bedroom door and watched as her mother dragged a suitcase from under the bed and opened it out. She yanked at the drawers in her dresser and began to throw her clothes, make-up, a bundle of papers and her jewellery into the case.

'Please don't go,' said Beth, her voice small, trembling.

Her mother bent down and kissed her cheek. 'As soon as I find a place to stay,' she said, 'I'll come back for you.' A horn sounded outside. Her mother stood up and looked around the room. 'This place is sucking the life from me. Your dad'll be home soon.' And then she was gone. The door slammed behind her, caught in the wind that howled up the strath like a living thing. It was a dark evening and rain ran sideways across the window glass.

7

A skeletal tree dipped and swayed outside, its branches clattering against the panes, a monster's arms reaching out, trying to break in, trying to reach the child.

Her father had not come home for hours, and when he did, she was huddled in a corner with her arms wrapped around her knees, her body racked from crying. He started to go to her, then saw the note his wife left. He read it, cursed and without speaking to his daughter, opened a bottle of whisky. Beth's memory of that evening was indelible, locked inside, echoing down all the years.

And she had waited for her mother, night after night, week after week, year after year, and somewhere deep in her heart, she was still waiting.

Chapter One

2014

Beth stepped off the bus at the top of Berriedale Braes under a sky piled grey upon grey. The first thing she noticed was the word, YES, painted in white on a towering rock on the hillside, a distance away yet plainly visible from the road. Someone else with their dreams in tatters, she thought. How long would it take for the letters to fade and be washed away by the force of time and elements? Quicker, no doubt, than the vision of independence would fade from many Scottish minds.

She remembered when she was five years old climbing from the school bus at this same spot and setting out alone under an immense sky. Now, all those years later, a memory slammed into her mind with remarkable clarity. With the memory came a rush of fear. She swallowed and took several deep breaths. At fifty-nine years old, a successful businesswoman with a career behind her, or so she appeared to the world, she had thought herself finally past the terrors of her youth.

Strands of hair blew around her face, the hair she had hated once, but now the hair for which she struggled to find the same shade of red in a bottle. She lifted her guitar case, eased the strap over her shoulder and thanked the driver.

As he removed the rest of her luggage from the baggage section, she looked around noting the changes to the countryside. Wind turbines dotted the hills and the bay, where, further out, the faded shapes of oilrigs were hardly discernible in a gathering sea mist. Modern bungalows replaced many of the small, sturdy cottages that once clung to the hillside like limpets to a rock. More than one had a 'For Sale' sign in the front garden.

The bus driver set Beth's case beside her, closed the door to the compartment and nodded at her feet. 'You won't get far up that road in those shoes, me girl.'

His accent was central London, startling her for a second, briefly reminding her of a time best forgotten. With a laugh at being called '*me girl'* by a man who was at least a decade younger than she was, she considered the rutted track before her and murmured, 'You're right. I should have remembered.' She opened her suitcase, removed a pair of flats and exchanged them for her high heels.

'Okay. Here goes,' she said to no one and, avoiding the branches of gorse that reached towards her stockinged legs, she set off along the side road to her father's cottage. Her case, balanced on its two wheels, jolted behind her, her steps in time with the beat of her heart. The only other sounds were the birds and the sea and the distant bleat of sheep.

After so many years in the city, the mountains to the south, the burn coursing through the glen dashing its spray upwards as it met the resistance of stone, the snaking road winding up the opposite hill, were almost foreign to her, yet startlingly familiar. Memories leaked from the cupboard at the back of her mind, drifting in like the ribbons of haar that twisted up the strath in the world of her childhood.

She saw herself as a skinny five-year-old walking along this same road, her hair pleated, her face scrubbed so that the skin stung; her school clothes immaculately pressed, her shoes brushed. Even then she knew that, as a plain child, she had to be a disappointment to a woman who looked like Veronica MacLean.

The cottage where she grew up sat about one and a half miles from the bus route, along a neglected track that led through heather and bracken. By the time she reached it, she was out of breath and the sky had begun to miserably spit rain.

The key lay heavy in her hand and chattered against the lock like cold teeth. Only then did she realise how badly she was shaking. At last the door creaked open, filling the silence with a scream of dry hinges. The odour of decay came out to meet her. Nothing appeared to have changed since the day she left. The old range with a one-bar electric fire set in front; the gas cooker, splatterings of grease on top and down the sides; lino on the floor, the pattern missing in places, but still bright in the corners where no feet ever trod; a moquette suite, one chair grimier than the others, the arms worn bare.

Now a layer of dust and evidence of mice coated everything, and the chill in the air, colder than outside, made her shiver. She wondered about her father living out his life in this cold box.

She should have come back sooner, should have come to see him when he was still well, not the emaciated figure she sat beside this morning in Raigmore Hospital in Inverness. The man she'd not seen for forty-two years before that.

Soon the house would be hers, the house, the ground, the memories that she could no longer contain. She flicked a switch and the bare lightbulb dangling from the ceiling threw its low wattage into the gloom. She went into the kitchen and gagged. Something left to rot. A half-empty tin of cat food sat on the draining board, mould growing on the surface. Opening the window to dispel the fetid air, she looked outside. The cat had probably found a home elsewhere by now, that or been eaten by foxes. Under the sink, she found half a bottle of bleach and set to work.

Some time later, satisfied that the kitchen was now as fresh as it could be, given the state and age of the building, she closed the window. The whole house could do with a good seeing to, but her muscles were already beginning to ache and she had broken two nails.

Her energy depleted, she ate the pot noodle she brought with her and drank a cup of instant coffee with powdered milk and no sugar. To someone used to eating meals cooked by a chef, it tasted vile. Then she went to the bedroom that was once hers. Inside, an onslaught of memories drifted within the shadows. Her single iron bed with the pink candlewick cover, her soft rabbit with the chewed ear sitting on top; the rose-flecked wallpaper, now yellowed at the corners and curling away from the plastered walls; the square of pink and grey carpet; her pine dressing table with the drawers that were difficult to open; the posters of Elvis, the Beatles, the Jackson Five, still tacked to the wall. Everything as she left it. But now, the room reeked of damp.

She stared at the bed. Probably a thousand crawling creatures had made their home there over the years. Beth crossed the landing to her father's bedroom and stopped, knuckling her eyes and filling her lungs with the sour air. Her father's bed was unmade, the indent of his head and a few stray hairs still on the pillow. She crossed to the cupboard and found clean sheets and blankets on the shelf where they always were. Somewhere in this house, she would find a hot water bottle, something to take the chill off.

On the second shelf sat a couple of tin biscuit boxes, slightly rusty at the edges. She lifted the first one and, taking it with her, sat on the bed and eased the lid off.

Surprised, she lifted a newspaper clipping, a grainy photo of herself at twenty-four, with the caption, **Hammond Signs New Hopeful**.

Beneath that, she found every report of her life, her rise to dubious fame, her fall. She quickly set them to one side and picked up a note, the note she penned on a page torn from her jotter on the day she left.

Dear Dad,

I'm going to London. I want to be a singer, and I know I'm just a nuisance to you anyway. I'll write when I get settled.

Beth

She smoothed the paper. Why had he kept this? He hadn't come after her as far as she knew. She hadn't expected him to.

Underneath that was the first letter she sent him, Edinburgh postmark, telling him that she was well and that she would never come home again. She had not added an address. Twenty years later she wrote another, one that her therapist encouraged her to send.

'Build bridges with your father,' the therapist said. *'He can give you the answers you need to know.'*

That time she *did* add an address.

He hadn't replied, but kept the letter. It was here, still in the envelope, the top edge jagged where it had been torn open. She tried not to think of her disappointment as she'd checked the mail day after day. Perhaps she should have returned then, tried to put right the wrongs of the past, but she'd been vulnerable, scarred. Her career as a singer was over and nothing else mattered.

Beneath that were her school reports, the father's day cards she made, the drawings she did at school, black and heavy. He'd kept them all.

At the bottom of the box was a photograph of her mother sitting on the dyke outside, head thrown back, mouth open in a laugh, her dark hair loose and tumbling down her back. And another, herself as a baby in her mother's arms. Her mother was gazing down at her with an expression of adoration. She studied the image, trying to recall the face, the dark hair, the red lips. 'Why did you leave me?' she asked. 'I needed you so much.' She thought her parents didn't love her, yet there was no mistaking the love in that photo. And her father, if she really was the burden she'd imagined herself to be, would he have followed her career so resolutely, kept every little memoir of her existence?

She removed the lid of the second box. The first thing she saw was a wedding photo of her parents, both in army uniform. Beneath that lay several snapshots, and a vision of a Box Brownie camera in her mother's hands flew through her mind. She picked up the picture of a baby in a gown assuming it was herself and turned it over. The name Michael was printed on the back. Michael? An unexplained frisson of fear worked its way up her spine. She shrugged it off. Who the hell was Michael?

Then another snapshot. This time of a boy of around five at her mother's side holding her hand. Quickly she leafed through the photos, photos she'd never seen before, and the boy featured in a lot. Michael aged one, Michael first day at school, Michael aged ten and Beth aged one. Michael sitting on an old-fashioned basket chair, a fat baby on his knee. Had she once had a brother? If so, why did she have no memory of him? Why did her parents never speak of him? Why had her father kept these photos from her?

After that, the only images she found were a couple of her school portraits. Michael was gone. And her mother was gone, and there were no more Box Brownie snapshots.

She found her parents' marriage certificate, her grandparents' death certificates. Nothing for Michael or herself.

'Who are you, Michael?' she said, but the silent face with the frozen smile mocked her from the photograph. A stranger, telling her nothing. A creak came from somewhere. Her fingers tightened on the image, her spine tingled. She imagined another's eyes upon her. She spun around. The room was empty as she knew it would be. An old house, settling and creaking. She forced a laugh at her own nervousness. Nevertheless, she thrust Michael's photos to the bottom of the pile, rose and left the room, gently closing the bedroom door, trapping the past and her memories behind it.

Later, sitting beside a blazing stove, glass of wine in hand, she tried to relax. The gale was a lost soul crying in the chimney. The house itself seemed to take a breath and release it with a tremble. The wind sighed and whistled. A cloud of smoke billowed into the room. Loose branches slapped against the windowpanes making her jump. It was just like that other night, that long-ago night. The night her mother left. And once again, she was in this house, alone.

For a moment she imagined the face of an eagle through the glass. She blinked, shook her head, rose and pulled the curtains blotting out whatever was out there.

For years she'd clung to the therapist's words explaining her nightmares.

You have come to see the eagle as a symbol of bad luck. You saw one that day, and that night your mother left.

There was no eagle, she told herself. There never had been. It was no more than an imaginary entity conjured

16

up by a lonely and unhappy little girl, an imaginary entity that grew and became something more, a vehicle for all the hurts of her young life. She set him free many years ago, released him, watched the imaginary eagle fly into an imaginary sky and take with him all her feelings of worthlessness. Why then, the constant sense that there was more?

Leaning against the wall she counted each breath until her heart stopped racing. Perhaps she should not have come back, should have left the past where it was. Done what Andy told her to do. There was reasonable accommodation in Inverness for the family of patients, yet she'd been drawn here by the same invisible bonds from which she once fought to escape. That, and the need to face the demons of the past, to finally convince herself that she stayed with Andy out of choice, not because of the deep-rooted fear of being alone.

She poured herself another glass of wine and drank it quickly, waiting as the welcome warmth spread through her body. From the corner came a scratching sound. Mice, she told herself, or worse still, rats, and she wondered again where the cat had gone. Apart from keeping the vermin down, she would have welcomed its company. Folded on the sofa was a tartan rug. She pulled it across her knees.

After the sounds of the city, the cottage felt dreadfully isolated. She had grown used to passing traffic, human voices in the street outside; music from the bar room; shouts of drunken merriment. All at once she wanted to hear Andy's voice, wished she had, after all, asked him to come with her. She picked up her phone and, realising

17

there was no signal, set it down again. Her father was ninety-three years old and lived all his life without a landline. The rug was thick and soft, and she guessed fairly new, and she snuggled within its folds and allowed herself to be lulled by the song of the wind.

She awoke, still on the couch, her head at a painful angle. The light outside was bright amber, the sounds were of the early morning; a seagull's cry, a bleating sheep, distant intermittent traffic. The empty wine bottle lay on the linoleum. She stretched, easing the cricks in her back, almost laughing at her fears of the night before. She glanced at her watch. Seven thirty. The cinders in the range still glowed, filling the room with a meagre warmth. Longing for a shower she went through to the bathroom to clean the bath. Brown water gushed from the hot tap, took minutes to clear, but remained cold. She had not thought to turn on the immersion heater. A wash-down was the best she could expect. In the kitchen, she switched on the kettle, mentally berating her father for not having the foresight to connect the water supply to the stove.

It occurred to her that if she was going to stay here for any length of time she would need a car. She'd left the Audi in Edinburgh with Andy. Two cars were a waste of money, he said, since he was on hand to drive her wherever she needed to be. For now, she would catch the early bus and spend some time by her father's bedside in the hope that he would recognise her, if for only a minute. She wanted him to see her, know she was there, forgive her.

Chapter Two.

A man sat in the bus shelter studying a newspaper. He was slim, with the rugged face of the outdoors and his white hair cut close to his head. Looking up as she approached, he smiled. 'Nice morning.' His voice was deep and soft and cultured.

She agreed as she sat down.

'I haven't seen you around before. Up on holiday?' He folded his newspaper and tucked it under his arm.

'I was brought up here,' said Beth, 'but I've been away a long time.'

His smile was easy, fluid, his eyes bright, perhaps too bright for a man who was no longer young.

'I only returned yesterday,' she added. 'The road's much improved since I was a child.'

'Still a tricky bend.' He held out his hand. 'I should know you, then. I'm James Anderson. My father used to be the local doctor for Berriedale and district.'

'Elizabeth MacLean, Beth to my friends. Are you a doctor too? Doctor Anderson?' The name was familiar, and the voice, she had heard it before.

A smile stretched his lips. 'I believe we've already spoken on the telephone. I was dragged out of retirement to act as locum for the local GP until a few days ago. I thought you should know about the old man.'

'Of course, Doctor Anderson. You contacted me to tell me about my father.'

'You weren't hard to track down.'

'Did you know him well, my father?'

James shook his head. 'Only met him a couple of weeks ago when I took over from Dr Montgomery, but he spoke about you a lot.'

'That surprises me.' Beth fell silent for a second. If the doctor found her so easily, her father could have as well, if he wanted to.

'You grew up here, then?' she said at last.

'Until I was eight. Then I was shipped off to boarding school. I vaguely remember Robbie MacLean's wee girl.'

'I don't recall much about school.' She studied his face, searching for something to recognise. Her school years hadn't been a happy time for her. The names, Carrot-top, Jug-ears, Dumbo, still stung. 'I think I do know you,' she said. 'The doctor's son, a big quiet lad who came home for the holidays.' She'd hardly noticed him. Thought of him as one of the 'posh' crowd, the crowd who wouldn't lower themselves to bother with the likes of her. And she didn't want him to remember her. The girl whose mother went off with another man, or so she'd heard it whispered, the girl no one wanted to be friends with.

'You were a bonny wee lassie, but awful feisty.' He gave a short laugh. 'I used to be afraid of you.' His gaze trapped hers.

'Afraid? Of me?' She forced a smile, realising he could never understand how much she had longed for friendship, how her anger had been her only defence. Thinking about the pain of her large ears, her frizzy hair, her freckled skin, she guessed he was being kind, that or confusing her with someone else. Self-consciously she tugged a strand of her hair, straightened this morning and already beginning to curl in the damp air. 'So you followed in your father's footsteps?'

'Sort of. I was a surgeon. Worked in Africa up until a few years ago. And you, you went on to be a pop star.'

She gave a short laugh, surprised that he'd even heard of her. 'I had my fifteen minutes of fame, yes. I did okay for a while.'

'I remember seeing you on the Old Grey Whistle Test on one of my trips home. I'd switched on to see Led Zeppelin, a favourite of mine, and there you were, appearing on the same show. You'd changed a lot, but I still recognised you right away.'

She smiled at the memory of that night. There was a last minute cancellation, and Lewis, her agent, called her. 'This is a good opportunity, girl,' he said. Her throat had been sore and it hurt to talk, but she went anyway.

'My wife bought all your records. Do you still sing?' James was still talking.

Beth paused and looked away from him and down into the strath. 'To be honest I grew tired of the life. I'm quite happy to keep it low key. Plus, well, I'm no longer young, as you can see.'

'You're still a good looking woman.'

She tugged at her hair. Although she'd had them surgically pinned back many years ago, she still tried to hide her ears in moments of self-consciousness,

'We own a club, in the centre of Edinburgh. It does very well.' She spoke quickly to cover her unexpected embarrassment.

'We?' His eyes fell to her left hand where she wore no wedding ring.

'I manage the musical side, hiring bands and acts. Andy, my partner, still plays guitar and sings during quiet periods and he takes care of the bar.' She didn't mention Glenda, the woman who helped with the day to day running of things. That name would have soured her tongue. 'We're not married, never saw the need.'

The chill of winter already tainted the air and she was glad to see the bus appear at the top of the brae.

'You're going to Inverness?' he said as he followed her onto the bus and took a seat beside her.

'To visit my father,' she replied.

'Of course. How is he?'

To her horror her eyes blurred. 'Some how we believe that our parents will be there forever. We never want to face the truth -- that they are growing very old. I can't get over the fact that he lay all night before the health visitor found him. If she hadn't come in... I should have come back...sooner.' She shook her head, unable to talk as emotion welled up, blocking her throat.

He set his hand on her arm. 'You're here now, that means a lot. He was a very private person.' James Anderson handed her a folded cotton handkerchief.

She nodded her thanks as her fingers closed around it. 'A real hanky. It's been a long time since I've seen anything other than tissues.'

'Call me a sentimental old fool,' he said with a slight laugh. 'My father always insisted that he had a newly pressed handkerchief every morning. It was a joke between my parents. Guess I've inherited the same streak. I never did come to terms with the paper kind — unless I've got a streaming cold of course.'

She stared through the window, not thinking of handkerchiefs. How could she tell him about the regrets, the lost years. She wondered how much he knew.

'It would be so much easier if he was in a local hospital,' she said, facing James again. 'Why was he sent to Inverness anyway?'

'They have more sophisticated equipment there.' James drew a breath. 'Caithness is a great place to live, but it has its drawbacks. If the powers that be had their way, everything would be in Inverness.' His voice rose, tense, angry. He rubbed his hands together and turned away from her. 'Don't get me on my soapbox about that one.'

'Do you live here now?' She changed the subject.

He cleared his throat and drew in some air. 'I came back when I retired. I bought the big house up on the hill.'

'The big house?' she asked, imagining all those rooms.

'Aye, I always admired it. Luckily it was for sale at the time I returned. Do you intend to stay?'

'I doubt it. Is your wife local?' Tucking a stray lock of hair beneath her ear, she met his eyes. They were deep blue. 'Would I know her?'

'My wife? No, and I'm afraid the marriage ended many years ago.'

'I'm sorry,' she muttered.

'Don't be. I'm not.'

'Caithness must be quite a change from Africa.'

'I always meant to come home one day. Buy a boat, a few sheep. This place pulls you back.'

23

Beth knew what he meant. She'd never intended to return, yet these last few years, she'd begun to feel that same pull. Was that what happened when you grew older? She thought of an elderly couple she knew, always reminiscing, lost in the past, but couldn't remember what day it was. She suddenly realised James was still speaking.

'I'm picking up my car from the garage.' He rose to leave the bus as it drew to a stop in Helmsdale. 'You know where I live. Give me a shout if you need anything.'

She watched him walk away, turning up the collar of his jacket. He was slim, broad shouldered with a sprint in his step that belied his years. He was nice, personable, and his chatter took her mind off her immediate worries for a while. She found herself hoping to meet up with James Anderson again. Anyway, she convinced herself, she wanted to know more about her father, but guessed, as a doctor, he would be gagged by some confidentiality clause or other.

Settling back, she closed her eyes, and her mind took her across the years to the last time she'd ridden the bus south. The road seemed longer then, more twists and turns, fewer bridges.

That day the bus did not appear to have any form of heating and she couldn't feel her feet. Her guitar was clutched on her lap, her woollen hat pulled down to her eyes and covering her ears, her long hair loose. She took out a packet of crisps, removed the little blue sachet of salt, emptied it onto the crisps and shook the bag vigorously. As she munched, she watched the passing countryside. It was raining, dull, slow drizzle, and the hills lay shrouded in grey. She tried not to think of her father's reaction when he read her note. He wouldn't be home until after seven and by then she would be in Edinburgh, probably sleep in the bus station, or get an overnight bus to London. Was there such a thing?

She heard his words in her head. 'Just like her mother. Just like her bloody mother. Well, good riddance, good riddance to both of them.' He would thump his fist on the table and pace the floor.

That day, she'd no real plan, but was carried away by the dream, the desire to leave the nothingness of her life and maybe, somewhere at the back of her consciousness, she hoped she would chance upon her mother. They would pass in the street, their eyes would meet and somehow, mother and daughter would instantly recognise each other. She banished that thought as quickly as it came. For years she'd tried to convince herself that she hated the woman who abandoned her.

Raindrops sloped across the windowpane, tears ran slowly down her cheeks, she was aware of her heartbeat and of a churning in her gut, and her overall memory was that of fear.

The bus pulled into the station in Inverness jolting her from her reverie. To her surprise, her cheeks were wet.

Chapter three

On the way to the ward, the sister told her that her father was awake and responding, but not to expect too much. He lay on his hospital bed in a side room, as if he hadn't moved from the position he'd been in the day before: his face as white as the pillow beneath his head, his mouth slightly open, a line of dribble on his cheek. He had a thin yellow tube attached to an arm and stuck down by a strip of clear, whitish tape, which puckered the papery skin. The tube threaded up to where a clear bag of fluid hung on a stand. The strong silent man who'd often carried her on his shoulders across the moors, who could shear more sheep in an hour than any crofter in the district, had gone and left this shell in his place. 'Dad,' she said, touching his arm. The arm was cold and still as if he were already dead. 'It's me, Beth.' She lowered herself onto the chair and shook his shoulder gently. His eyes opened and for a moment remained unfocused, then flickered across her face. She took his hand and the bones lay under the skin like brittle sticks making her afraid to apply any pressure. He became tense; the skeletal hand in hers began to shake.

'Nurse, nurse,' Beth shouted.

A nurse hurried over. 'It's all right, Robbie,' she said in a soothing voice as she checked his vital signs. 'This is your daughter, Beth.'

He seemed to sink into the bed.

'Speak to him.' The nurse turned to Beth. 'He is responding. I'm sure he understands, knows you're here.'

Beth wet her lips. 'Dad, do you know me?'

Cool fingers fluttered against hers, a vibration of twigs. And she recognised a forcing of dying muscles to respond.

'Oh, Dad,' she whispered, 'Is there something you want to say?'

His eyes moved across her face, but there was no hope in them.

'It's all right. I'm not going away again. There's so much I want to tell you.'

The twig-fingers fluttered.

'You'll be able to do more tomorrow. I'm sorry I left you.' And she was, sorry they'd never talked, that she'd never tried to understand. She stayed away because of anger; blaming him for all that was wrong in her life; blaming him for her mother leaving; blaming him for not caring enough to come looking for her. In any case her life had become so hectic, and somewhere at the back of her mind, she believed there would be time. A few days ago she received the phone call, and was hit by the realisation that there was no more time.

'I was so busy. And angry, and I shouldn't have been. When you're well enough, I'll take you home, look after you.' As she spoke she knew she would, for however long he had left.

She sat with him, telling him the parts of her life she was not reluctant to share, until she saw that he was sleeping. 'I'll be back tomorrow, Dad,' She kissed his brow. It was dry and cool.

Leaving the hospital, she turned on her phone. Andy. Three missed calls. She dialled her answering service.

Beth, where are you? Are you alright? Call me back as soon as you get this.

With a deep sigh, she punched in his number.

'It's me,' she said, when she heard his voice.

'Beth. I've been worried sick.'

She quickly explained why he hadn't got through. 'And there's no service in the mountains, or patchy, so don't worry. I'm fine.'

'I won't manage up till the weekend. I'll come then, but if you need me, I'll just leave everything and I'll be right there.'

'No, no don't come up. I'm coping fine, honest. I'm just going to do some shopping and head back to the cottage.' She swallowed her irritation without knowing what irritated her. Andy was good to her, wasn't he? Had always known what was best for her, so why did she feel this way? Although she knew that in her low moments the temptation to call him, have him hold her and tell her he would take care of everything, would be strong, she had no real desire for his cloying presence. Being on her own these last couple of days had given her a barely remembered sense of freedom.

'Beth, are you still there? I said, how's your father?'

She started.

'No real change. Look, Andy, I'm staying here as long as he needs me. And you don't have to be here, honest. We can't both neglect the club.'

'You're really fine aren't you? I mean you'd tell me if anything was wrong, wouldn't you?'

She snorted. 'I'm not crazy, Andy. And I don't have a problem with alcohol, whatever you say. In fact, I'm going to confront my ornithophobia. See, I can even pronounce that word now.' She laughed, a little too shrilly. 'I'm going to the Wild Life Park in the Black Isle and I'm going to get close up to some big birds, how's that?' The words fell into her mind as if from the air around her.

He gave a snort of derisive laughter. 'You?' And then he seemed to catch himself. 'Are you sure?'

'Certain, Andy, I'm fine.' Why did he always do that? Make her feel inadequate, doubt her own judgement?

'Call me the minute you need me, hear?'

'I will. Talk to you soon.' She rang off. No, she decided, she did not want him here. This was one journey she had to make alone.

Chapter Four

It had been early spring, 1973 and Andy McRae was trying to earn enough money to stay another year at university. His father died the year before and his mother was finding life hard. True he had the grant, but Edinburgh was expensive, especially so for students from the Western Isles who couldn't pop home easily at the weekends. He had been busking at the entrance to Waverley Station and doing fairly well, but tonight there was a young girl sitting in his spot strumming a cheap acoustic guitar which was slightly out of tune.

His first reaction was anger. This was a good spot and it was his. He was about to ask her to move on when she began to sing. Her voice was soft and slightly husky and unbelievably beautiful. She didn't see him. Her head was lowered. Her straggly reddish hair hung around her face, a woollen hat pulled down covering her ears and eyebrows. She wore jeans, wide round the bottoms and a parka over a loose shirt, a string of coloured beads around her neck. Totally captivated, he stood there until the song finished. Later he would tell her that he fell in love with her the moment she lifted her head and he became aware of a pair of grey-green eyes that held a wealth of sadness.

He wanted to say, 'Excuse me, you're in my pitch,' instead, the words, 'Your guitar needs tuning,' fell unbidden from his mouth.

'I know that. But I don't have a tuning fork with me,' she replied.

He sat beside her, opened his guitar-case, withdrew a fork, and held out his hand for her instrument. Wordlessly she handed it to him. Once he finished, she nodded a thank you and listened as he began to strum out a tune of his own.

Together they played, with him singing the harmony to her songs. After a while a crowd gathered and after each song there was applause. A couple of hours later, Andy set his guitar down. 'I'm going for something to eat,' he said, gathering up the tin with the money, meaning to share it.

She snatched at it. 'That's mine,' she shouted. 'I didn't ask you to join me.'

He immediately let go and held up his hands. 'Okay, okay, actually this is my spot.'

Her face reddened. 'You don't own a piece of pavement,' she snapped. 'And I was here first.'

'Fine, you keep it.'

Her lip wobbled. She trapped it between her teeth and lowered her eyes but not before he saw the tears shimmering there.

He melted. 'You're good. How do you fancy joining my group?' The words tumbled out without thought.

Her head rose, she sniffed and wiped her cheeks. Her smile was like the sun breaking through a cloud. 'You've got a group?'

'A duo actually. We're playing in a bar tonight. You could come with us.' It occurred to him that Desmond would object, he should have run it by him first, but something vulnerable about the girl pulled at his heartstrings and he knew right then that he wanted to keep her near. Furthermore, Andrew McRae was used to getting his own way. Desmond always gave in in the end. 'Where do you live?' he asked.

She shrugged. 'I just got here yesterday. I've no had time to sort something out.'

'Where did you sleep last night?'

'In the station.'

He bent down and picked up her rucksack. 'Come back with me. You'll sleep in my flat for now.'

Snatching at her rucksack, she faced him with narrowed eyes. 'I'll be fine,' she said. 'I don't need no boy to do me favours!'

'No strings attached.' He released the bag. 'You'd be helping me out by singing with us, really. We're musicians, my buddy and me, but we need a strong vocalist.'

She still looked wary. 'I'll no be able to pay rent.'

He laughed. 'With a voice like you've got, you will be, I promise.'

Desmond did object. Loudly. 'For God's sake, man. There's no enough room here for the two of us. And the group's just us, you and me.'

'I didn't want to come anyway.' Beth wiped her nose on the back of her fingerless glove, slung her rucksack over her shoulder and headed for the door. Andy got there before her, slamming his hand against it, holding it shut.

'You're staying, no argument.' He turned to face his friend. 'She can stay in my room, share my food.' His voice rose. 'But for fuck's sake listen to her sing, man, just listen to her sing.'

Desmond turned away. 'I don't care how good she is. She'll be trouble. How old is she? She looks like jailbait. She's probably a runaway. I don't need any grief. My old man would stop my allowance, ' he clapped his hands together, 'Just like that.'

'Please, mate,' said Andy, 'She's every damn bit as good as Marianne Faithfull, if not better.'

Desmond lifted and lowered his hands in a gesture of defeat. 'I'll listen. But then she goes.'

Beth swung her guitar from her back and strummed a tune they had not heard before. She began to sing.

You've come a long way from the mountains
Where the cold wind blows
And the sun don't shine
But somewhere in the future you'll find her
In a cold dark place,
Will she still chase
The dream she left behind her

By the time she finished, tears were streaming down her face. Andy would never have admitted it, but he swallowed a lump in his own throat.

Desmond opened his eyes wide. 'Wow,' he said. 'Where did you hear that song?

'I wrote it,' said Beth dabbing at the dampness on her cheeks. 'Did...did you like it?'

'Like it, I love it. Wow, girl, you *are* good.'

'Then she can stay?' asked Andy.

'Hold on there, I didn't say that. We're hardly making enough to keep ourselves, less if we've got to split it three ways.'

'I don't need paying,' said Beth. 'A place to stay and I'll busk for food. And... and I'll cook for you.' She didn't say then that her speciality was toast. Toast with baked beans, toast with sardines, toast with sloppy scrambled eggs. She turned and glared at Andy. 'And I won't be sharing your bed!' she added.

Andy held out his hands, palms facing her. 'Bloody hell, I said my room, not my bed. No strings, remember?'

Desmond still looked undecided.

'I'll do the washing too.'

'Come on, man. Give it a try, what can we lose?' said Andy.

Desmond sighed. 'The cooking bit sounds good.'

How were they to know then the limits of her cooking skills?

He turned to Beth. 'Welcome to the Andy and Des Duo. At least for tonight, it'll be Des, Andy and friend. We'll see how it goes.'

'Bloody terrible name,' said Andy. 'How about Andy, Beth and Desmond?'

'How about Beth and friends?' Beth immediately chipped in.

'I told you a girl would be trouble,' said Desmond, but he was smiling. 'Look, I'm agreeing to nothing. If we're booed tonight, she's out.'

That night they totally won over the audience at the World's End bar. A week later the bookings were flooding in. A month later, the boys gave up their studies to go into music full time. It was the days of rock n' roll, yet Beth refused to sing anything other than folk songs. 'My voice is wrong for rock and roll,' she said, and although they never hit the big time, they became well-known in their own field.

Andy poured himself a whisky, walked to the office window and looked down into the busy street below. Beth. He could still see her now as she had been then. She was never classically beautiful, but she possessed a spark that dulled any other woman in her company. Yet for all her bravado, he grew to see, beneath the façade, the vulnerable, frightened little girl who sang with tears pouring down her cheeks.

Over the years, her confidence in her own musical ability grew, but he would never forget that first night in the World's End bar.

'I can't go on,' she said.

'What?' Andy couldn't believe his ears.

She wiped her brow. 'All those people, I can't face them.' Her freckles stood out against her pale skin. Her lip trembled. 'I'm sorry. I can't.'

'What the hell now?' Desmond rolled his eyes and shrugged.

'You sang all afternoon, in the street for fuck's sake! I persuaded Desmond...'

'That was different. Now there's... there's an... audience, and no one will listen. I need a drink.'

It was true, the audience had chatted all the way through the last act.

'Just leave her, man. Put her back where you found her,' said Desmond.

'I'll get you something. What do you want?' Andy felt his anger grow, bubbling under the surface. She couldn't humiliate him now.

'Vodka. And coke. A double.'

She took the drink with a trembling hand and swallowed it in three gulps.

'We're on,' he said. 'Now get out there or I'll boot your arse.'

She looked at him with fear in her eyes and for a moment he thought she was going to refuse. She wobbled slightly as he shepherded her before him onto the stage. Another awkward moment as he started to strum. Beth stared at the floor, the microphone held unsteadily in her hand. Her voice started weakly, and as he glowered at her he saw a transformation take place. She lifted her head, her voice grew strong. Suddenly it was as if no one else existed. She sang for herself, wrapped in her own island, eyes and cheeks glistening. The crowd fell silent, and when the song ended, the applause could have lifted the roof.

As time went on, the trio grew restless. They found the confines of local gigs no longer satisfied them. They dreamed of cutting a record that would shoot them to fame. And then Lewis Hammond came into their lives. The man who was to rip their world apart.

Andy stomped to his desk and refilled his glass. He could well remember that time, the first time she left him. And he would not suffer a repeat performance now.

He had let her go then. He even forgave her, took her back afterwards. He gave a wry laugh. Lewis Hammond. He promised to make her into a star, but demolished her in the process. She promised to take Andy with her on the ladder to success, promised him he could be her manager, like Cilla Black and Bobby. How mistaken he had been to trust her.

Lewis Hammond. Even now, the name made Andy's body tighten. And the pain of Beth's betrayal still stung.

He steadfastly followed her career. She made records that reached the top ten, she sang on Top of the Pops. She was on her way up. Then came the botched operation that stole her voice. Lewis Hammond was reported as saying she was a liability and he washed his hands of her, and as quickly as she had risen to fame, she faded like yesterday's news. Andy swallowed his pride and and forgave her, at least with words. How was he to know her voice had gone for good?

When she returned to him, she was a shadow of the feisty girl she once was. Alcohol and drugs dulled the pain of her loss and diminished her bank account. He brought her home and nursed her back to health. He asked her to marry him once, but she'd turned him down, swearing she'd never marry anyone. Nevertheless, he held her when she cried about things best forgotten, and finally convinced her that she needed looking after, looking after by him. Even then he believed that her voice would return, that this was just a temporary setback, and this time *he* would manage her career. But he had been wrong. She refused to even try to sing again in public. Accepting defeat, his ambitions changed direction. The royalties from her songs still arrived and she owed him.

That had been years ago. Since then they bought the club and become lovers, but he hated it that when he held her he sensed her distance, as if he possessed her body but never her heart. He often caught her with a faraway look on her face, a tear in her eye and he suspected she stayed with him only because he supplied the stability she craved.

They enjoyed a comfortable lifestyle. Beth still had contacts. She booked many big-name bands that drew in the crowds. Andy McRae's club made him a name in the city.

His hand closed into a slow fist as his mind whirled, consumed with a new fear of losing her, hating that she had never really been his.

Glenda, an employee, a bit of an all-rounder, who helped him in the bar, Beth with the administration, and who ran the kitchen, moved past him, brushing him with her thigh as she did so, startling him from his daydreaming. She turned, met his eye and smiled.

'Penny for them,' she said, her voice low, seductive.

Andy rose from the office chair. He walked to the window and looked out onto the grey street. 'Have we got a group lined up for tonight?'

'I've tried a few, but they're all booked up. Look, I meant to ask you, my sister's boy is good on the guitar. It would be great if you would give him and his friends a chance.'

Andy sighed. 'We need a known name to pull in the crowds.'

'Darren's really good. It's the best I could do at such short notice.' She trailed a suggestive finger across his shoulder. Andy swallowed, felt his Adam's apple bob. He groaned and grabbed her hand. 'Don't do that. Business and pleasure, remember?'

She pulled her hand away from his, walked slowly to the door swinging her hips, and turned the key. 'The door's locked,' she whispered. 'Beth doesn't deserve you. I could make you happy.'

He groaned. 'No, Glenda.'

Bristling, she drew back. 'What's wrong with me? It's not as if you've not cheated on Beth before.'

'There's nothing wrong with you, but I don't shit on my own doorstep.' His voice was gruff. He closed his eyes against the temptation. She was lovely, sexy, seductive, but he knew the dangers of playing with fire.

Chapter Five

Once back home, Beth dumped the shopping bags on the draining board and lit the stove. By now the water should be hot enough for a bath. She prepared herself a meal of ready-cooked chicken and salad and put some frozen chips in the oven to cook. While she waited, she wandered through to her father's bedroom and stripped off his bedding. After making up the bed, she sat in front of the dressing-table for a few minutes rest.

Lifting her head, she caught her reflection in the mirror and imagined her child-face staring back at her. She had loved sitting here surrounded by her mother's things. Her perfume, her lipstick and rouge, her soft-smelling face powder in the box with the pretty lid.

'Mother of pearl,' Veronica told her, allowing the child to run her fingers over it. 'It'll be yours one day.' And she picked up her hairbrush. 'Let's brush each other's hair.'

The pleasant memory faded. Beth rubbed her eyes and rose to her feet.

Downstairs, she ate her meal, took a bath and dressed in her nightclothes. A glass of wine and the heat from the stove made her drowsy, the wind outside brought back fluttering wings of memory. In an effort to keep them at bay, she rubbed her hands together, lifted her guitar and began to strum. Her fingers were no longer as supple as they needed to be for professional playing. Andy had been right to persuade her to buy that club. She began to sing, something she only did when she was alone. She chose a song she wrote years ago, the song that took her into the charts.

I wish I could go back to what I used to be.
A simple little girl, so innocent and free.
Somewhere along life's path, much has been lost and
little gained.
Somewhere along life's path, it has rained.

Frustrated by a voice that could no longer hit the high notes, she set her guitar aside, wiped her cheeks and poured another drink, emptying the bottle. Why did she keep trying to sing? Did she really think that one day a miracle would happen?

Back in her other existence, singing had been her world, filling up the empty places. And it wasn't just the songs; she revelled in the adoration of her fans and the applause that electrified her. She loved the life, the money, the parties, aah, the parties. And Lewis. Rat that he turned out to be. He had swept her off her feet with his promises, his suave good looks, his flashy cars, his elaborate lifestyle, his guarantees of fame and fortune. He made her over and turned her into a star and she forgot her promise to Andy and Desmond to find them a job in the industry once she had her foot on the ladder. When she overtook Leo Sayer in the charts, it filled her with a false sense of her own importance. And then, one morning it hurt to swallow. The doctor warned her of the dangers of straining her vocal cords. He told her to cancel her next concert, her next tour, to stop smoking, and she ignored him, forcing the songs from her heart even when the very notes that gave her life caused shooting pains from ear to ear. Eventually she was diagnosed with polyps on her vocal chords. They coarsened her voice making it less than perfect. Encouraged by pressure from Lewis, she agreed to have the offending growths removed.

Hammond had a friend, a surgeon who, he said, once ran a practice in Harley Street, and she trusted his choice. But the knife did more harm than good. The damage was irreversible. She soon realised it had all been smoke and mirrors, none of it was real. She was a voice, not a person at all. As her fickle fans found another idol, Hammond dropped her for a new protégé, and Beth the pop star disappeared. When she caught him in bed with his latest conquest and he laughed at her hurt, she took solace in alcohol and drugs that filled the void as her dream faded.

One night, alone and drunk, nursing the feeling that she had nothing left to live for, she called Andy.

'It's Beth,' she slurred, when he answered. There was a long silence.

'I understand you won't want to talk to me.' She hung up and started to cry in earnest. She had lost everything, everyone. For a long time she stared at the bottle of sleeping tablets on her bedside cabinet. Then her thoughts turned to Berriedale and her father. If he'd only installed a telephone. But she could call the local hotel, they would get a message to him. She reached out her hand and as she did so, the telephone rang.

'Hello.' She pressed the receiver to her ear.

'Beth, where are you?'

'Andy... Andy I'm so sorry... you were right... I shouldn't have gone...' Her voice failed her and she dissolved into a new fit of weeping.

'Tell me where you are and I'll come and get you,' he said.

Gratitude overwhelmed her. Gratitude that still bound her to him after all this time.

The first night he took her home to his one-bedroom flat in Haymarket, he treated her as if she was made of glass. He gave her his bed and made up the sofa for himself. At the time he was working as a manager for a hardware store and singing in a dingy bar room at the weekends. He had had a lady friend, he told her, but that had recently ended.

'Don't worry,' he said. 'I'll soon have you back to normal. Lots of sleep and good food. I eat most nights at the café on the corner. Mario makes the best pasta dishes outside Italy! Your voice'll soon come back, you'll see.'

'It won't,' she said. But he ignored her, and gradually lost patience with her despondency.

A few weeks later, when he came home to find her still in her dressing gown, he heaved open the curtains and uttered a snort of disgust. 'It's about time you got yourself out of this state,' he said. 'I can't go on keeping you for nothing. I promised the lads you'd come with us on Saturday night. And no more of this.' He snatched the cigarette out of her hand and threw it into the bin. 'They don't do your voice any good.'

'I told you, I can't sing.' Wounded by his harsh words, she rose and pushed her fingers through her tangle of hair.

43

'Won't sing, you mean. It's all in the mind, Beth.'

'If that's the only reason you took me back, I wish I'd stayed away.'

'I'm beginning to wish that too.' He stormed out of the flat slamming the door, and she didn't see him for several days. When he did come back he was sheepish. 'Look Beth, I told one of my friends about you. She thinks you should talk to someone, a professional.'

'You spoke about me to a stranger?' She couldn't believe this.

He ran his hand over his head. 'There's the drinking. And the nightmares.'

'What drinking? I've never touched a drop since I've been here. And I've always had nightmares when I'm stressed, and you telling me I can sing if I try is stressing me no end.'

'Come off it. It's only a matter of time before you fall off the wagon and you haven't had a decent fucking night's sleep since you came back. And neither have I. Look, I've managed to get an appointment with a therapist. Not cheap, but it'll be worth it to see you back to what you were.'

'For God's sake, will you listen. My vocal chords are damaged. My voice is weak. It's not going to happen.' She stormed into the bedroom, pulled her holdall from under the bed and started throwing her clothes into it.

'What are you doing?' shouted Andy, grabbing her arm.

'You're like all the rest. You just want me to make money for you. Well, get this through your thick skull, the golden goose is laying no more eggs!' She jerked away from him.

His voice lowered. 'Aw, come on. I didn't mean it like that. Where are you going to go? Look, I won't pressure you anymore, honest. Just see this doctor, what harm can it do?'

She suddenly felt the strength drain from her legs and she sank down onto the bed. It was true she had nowhere to go, and she did need help. Her life had become a mess. 'And you'll stop going on about me singing?'

His hand made a crossing motion on his chest, but his eyes remained unconvinced.

Doctor Madelaine, as she called herself, did help her. She even helped to convince Andy that Beth's loss of voice was physical. But, as the layers of her past began to peel away, the nightmares became worse. It was then he decided the therapy was a waste of money.

She had been happy enough to leave, although it was against the advice of Doctor Madelaine. There was a door in her mind that she was scared to open, and without Andy's support, she could not go there.

Finally accepting that her voice loss was permanent, Andy came up with the idea of the club and she welcomed it. It gave her the opportunity to surround herself with the life she was no longer part of.

She continued to write songs for a while, but unable to find a market for her stuff, she turned to poetry, deep meaningful lines into which she poured her heart and soul.

Lost in the past, she closed her eyes and allowed herself to be comforted by the settling of the fire, the whistle of the wind outside and the faded music in her head.

Suddenly the eagle sat before her, his great wings folded against his sides, his eyes yellow. He did not speak, at least in the way Beth knew, with voices that splintered the air. His voice was the voice of the wind, the voice of the river running through the glen fast and furious with the swell of spring and melting snow.

'I am your friend,' he said. But she knew he lied. She knew he had come to seek revenge. He moved closer and the face filled her vision, the scent of the mountains filled her nostrils, and she heard the beat of his heart matching her own. The hooked beak brushed her shoulder. She closed her eyes waiting for the slash to her throat. It never came.

And then he had gone. She watched him spread his wings and rise into the sky, higher and higher, and the terror filling her heart slipped away. The wind was cold on her cheeks and she shivered, the loneliness of her early life closing in on her. 'Mammy,' she cried.

She woke with a start. The curtains, flapping like the wings of a bird, reached towards her. The rising wind filled the room. The window was swinging open. She rose and pressed it closed against the determined gale. Immediately behind her something crashed. She spun around, eyes flying first to the floor where a ceramic lady that had once belonged to her father's grandmother, lay shattered on the lino. Then her eyes swept up to the sideboard. A large, grey cat stood there its back arched, its ears flattened, its slitted eyes hard and yellow. Her body went soft as relief soaked through her.

'Puss,' she cried, holding out her hand. The cat lifted its round head, lowered its back, yet still eyed her suspiciously. Finally, as if deciding she could be trusted, it purred and meowed. She walked forward and he butted the offered hand.

'Sorry, puss,' she said. 'I've no cat food. But I think I've some chicken left over.'

The cat fell on the chicken as if it hadn't eaten for days. When she finally lowered herself onto the settee there was a sense of comfort at the warm body pressing itself against her leg, paws kneading her thigh, a contented rumble in the animal's throat. They had always had cats when she was a child, and dogs. She had wanted a pet, but Andy was allergic to cats, and, living in a flat with busy working lives, it would have been unfair on a dog.

The window swung open again. The curtains streamed towards her. The cat arched its back and growled. Beth rose quickly, checked the latch, closed the window and checked the latch again. It seemed secure enough. A chill ran the length of her spine. She thought of James. She would go and see him tomorrow, see if he knew any joiners in the area; if she got locks fitted, that would do it, she thought.

As if compelled, she reached for her pad and pencil and started a new poem. 'To an Eagle.'

In dreams,
Gliding, poised,
Muscles straining,
Feathers unruffled against the wind,
Head angled.
Below, where grass shivers,
Scurrying innocence
Is marked for extinction.
Caught in the evil of your eye.

She reread it, drew a single line through it and started again. Once she was as happy with her words as she could be, she felt calm enough to search for sleep.

She woke early after a restless night and padded into the kitchen, checking the windows as she went. All were secure. Taking her coffee cup with her, she walked out into the early morning. The sun was soft, bright and low. The river dashed in ropes of white and pewter through the glen, between trees splendid in their autumnal colours. In the months of spring these hills would become a riot of yellow where the broom spread over the mountain. On a morning like this, it was hard to imagine the lashing storms of winter.

'I'll be away this afternoon,' she told the cat. 'But I'll be back in time for tea.' She bent down and scratched behind one battle-scarred ear and tried not to think of windows that opened of their own accord in the night.

She found James standing at his front door looking down the glen. He was unshaven, slightly heavy eyed, and wore a cable jumper the colour of sheep's wool. In the

48

glen, the haar, a soft white blanket of mist that crept landward during the hours of darkness, had not yet fully cleared. He glanced up as she approached. 'I never tire of the scenery round here,' he said. 'Every season a different picture. Come in, come in.' He led her into a large, littered kitchen with an iron range against the far wall, the furniture stately and old, reminiscent of another era.

James cleared away a pile of books from a chair. 'Sit down. Coffee? I was just going to make my first cup of the day.' Lifting a cafetière from the draining board, he rinsed it under the tap.

'Yes please,' she said.

'So what brings you here? Not that you're not welcome at any time.' He was looking at her over his shoulder as he spoke.

'I need to buy a car. Something reasonable. I wondered if you knew of anything?'

He set the cafetière down and crossed to his laptop on the table. There was a ping of Microsoft Windows loading. 'I'll have a look on Caithness.org. We might pick up something. Here,' he turned the screen to face her. 'Browse that lot while I get the coffee.'

She chose a couple of private sales that sounded promising.

'I'll take you there this afternoon. Milk and sugar?'

'Just milk. No need to take me. I can bus it,' she said.

'I insist.'

'And the catch on the living room window needs fixing. I wondered ...'

'I can look at that for you too.'

'I didn't mean... I wondered if you knew a handyman.'
She shrugged.

'Right here.' He pointed to his chest.

'That's good of you. I'll pay of course.'

'Not at all. Just have dinner with me, okay?' He lifted his eyebrows.

'Sure. I'll even make it. I'm a fair cook if I need to be.' Why did she say that? With her cooking skills, he'd be lucky to get beans on toast.

'I'll look forward to it.' James' smile was wide and lit up his face. A smile she could trust. And she realised she was smiling, too.

She turned her coffee cup around, serious now. 'James,' she began, 'when we were children, what do you remember about my family?'

'Not a lot. I remember you in school, that's about it.'

'There are things I need to know, things no one told me.'

'What things?'

'I don't remember much before my mother left. But there were photos in the house, photos I'd never seen before. A boy I don't know. I think I may have had a brother, maybe he died when I was young, but I've no memory of him.'

James shrugged. 'I don't remember you having a brother. We could ask my mother about your family. She lives in Lybster. We'll drop in when I take you to see the cars. Mind you, she's a bit forgetful now, tends to ramble on sometimes.'

Beth finished her coffee, rose and walked to the window. A roe deer stood in the garden outside and,

50

without fear, he continued chewing and studied the face behind the glass. 'Bambi,' she said beneath her breath. She had forgotten the deer.

James came up behind her. 'He comes most days. I sometimes get red deer, and rabbits, lots of rabbits and hares. They seem almost tame, as if they know I wouldn't hurt them.'

For a long moment they stood like that, in silence, until, as if alerted by an invisible predator, the deer started and sprung away, leaving the garden empty. Beth's eyes flicked to her father's cottage nestled in the folds of the opposite hill.

'I'd love to meet your mother,' she said, turning back towards the room.

Nettie Anderson lived in a small bungalow, just off the main street in Lybster village. She was a round, warm woman who gave Beth a welcome that made her wish she could stay there forever. Shuffling rather than walking, she led them into a bright chintzy living room and served them tea poured from a china teapot into china cups with saucers. She brought out a matching plate of shortbread and chocolate biscuits. 'If James had told me sooner that you were coming, I'd have done a baking,' she said, eyeing Beth and frowning. 'You're awful pale and thin. Eat up now.'

'Mother, don't get personal,' said James.

Beth's slimness was a source of pride to her when so many women her age found it difficult to shift the extra pounds. 'It's fine,' she said to James, then looked at Nettie. 'This is lovely, thank you.' She couldn't remember when she'd last drunk tea from a china cup and she thought it tasted better somehow.

'James said you wanted to ask me some things. You'll have to speak clear though. Folk nowadays either shout or mumble.' She adjusted her hearing aid and it made a screeching noise. She grimaced and pulled it out. 'Just talk clear, I'm no deaf.'

Beth caught James' eye and he smiled indulgently.

She leaned forward and cleared her throat. 'Do you remember my family?'

'I mind Robbie MacLean. Quiet lad. He was called up when the war started. I mind seeing him in his uniform before he left. I was just a bairn at the time, no more than nine or ten. What a bonnie looking young man he was. His hair was red, like yours. All gone now I expect.'

'And later, after the war, do you remember my mother?'

'He didn't come back here after the war. They settled somewhere else for a while. They came back... She stared at the far wall, 'about '53 or '54. Ach, My memory's no what it was.' She smiled, her eyes distant, lost in the past. 'I was aye good at figures. Top o' my class at school. But we never had the chances then they have nowadays. Could have gone further, you ken. Gone to university, my teacher said. But I had to leave school, gut the herring for very little pay. There were twelve of us. I was the youngest, the only one alive now. It was a hard life back then, but good, can't say it wasn't good.' She stopped, a smile tugged her lips. 'I married well.' She looked at James. 'He came here as a young man. All the lassies were after the new doctor, I swear, there was

52

more illness all of a sudden than there ever was before! You look so like him, son. Many a time...'

'What about Beth's mother?' said James, bringing her back.

'Oh, aye, well, like I was saying, she was a right bonny lassie, your mam. You've a good look of her, except for your hair. I saw her in the shop sometimes. She kept you lovely, like a wee doll with your golden curls. Never saw you again once she left. Gladys Mitchell, that was your schoolteacher, she tried to take an interest, spoke to your dad, but he told her to mind her own business. They said he went clean to pieces after your ma left, let himself go right downhill. There was many that would have helped him, especially with the bairn, but he didn't want it. But he doted on you, though, I'm sure he did.'

Beth had never felt doted on. She wet her lips. 'Do you ever remember a boy living in my house?'

Nettie shook her head. 'When your mam and dad moved here they only had the one bairn. That would be you.'

'So I was born somewhere else?' She stopped for a moment while she digested this. 'Have you any idea where we lived before?'

'I don't know, love. I'm sorry I can't help you more, but I hardly knew your family. Your granddad died and your dad came back to run the croft, I heard. We lived in Dunbeath by then. Your mam was from the city and I heard them say that she'd never really settled in the country.'

53

'Who would know? Is there anyone who was a friend or neighbour?'

'They were a quiet couple, kept themselves to themselves. No one knew much about them. Didn't want anyone to know.' She lifted her hand. 'Wait, she sang in a band. A Scottish dance band, just for a couple of months before she left. They said she left with the drummer. Oh, I'm sorry...' She put her hand over her mouth.

'No, no, go on. She... she sang? Are any members of the band still around?'

Nettie shook her head and gave a little laugh. 'Och no, for they were all a good bit older than her. The drummer, he was a younger man, came from the south. Never heard her myself, but they say she was very good.'

'What about the teacher, Gladys Mitchell?'

'Ach, sorry, lass, Gladys passed on last summer.' She set her hand on Beth's. 'I wish I could help you more. But come back and see me, I'll bake next time.'

'Aye, I'll do that,' said Beth, her face relaxing into a smile.

'Thanks, Mother,' said James. 'But we'll have to go. We're going to John O' Groats to look at a couple of cars. Don't get up, we'll see ourselves out.'

'I hope your dad gets better.' Nettie looked up at Beth. 'And do come back.'

Beth thanked the old woman again as they headed for the door, her mind already racing. All her life she'd ignored the need to find out about her past, never had the time anyway, why should she let it bother her now? Andy's voice came back to her.

'You don't need your family. What have they ever done for you? I'm here now, I love you and I'll never leave you.'

Maybe he was right. She managed to deny any curiosity she might have had for most of her life, even gave up on therapy when the questions hit a nerve, and threatened to remove the ability to banish all thoughts from her mind. Some places were too painful to visit.

Andy never gave up on her, did he? Even after she fell hopelessly, madly in love with Lewis Hammond, so much so she would have done anything he asked of her and almost did. She believed he felt the same way about her until she caught him in bed with another up and coming starlet. That was the night she went on stage the worse of alcohol. Her voice had not only been weak and hoarse from the operation, but slurred, the audience weaving before her eyes. She shuddered at the memory. There was no clapping that night, only jeers and boos. She went to her dressing room and trashed it.

'You okay?' James brought her back to the present. 'You were miles away.' He opened the passenger door for her.

'Yes, I'm fine. Someone walked over my grave.' She forced a little laugh, and wiped an unexpected tear from her eye.

John O'Groats had changed since she'd last been here. Chalets filled the field behind a shopping precinct, which appeared to have sprung up, flourished and died during her absence. The hotel where her father once took her for high tea was under renovation.

'Everything changes,' she said, as she stood on the shore looking over the firth towards the islands to the north, shivering under the onslaught of a northerly breeze. 'Come on,' she said, 'I'll treat you to a coffee, then we'll go buy a car.'

The car she chose, a small Punto, was in good condition and within her price range. She shook the seller's hand and wrote out a cheque, surprised that he let her take the Punto then and there, not waiting for the cheque to clear as would have happened in the city.

'I need to get some shopping on the way home,' she told James. 'I'll see you at seven for dinner.'

He saluted. 'I'll look forward to it.'

She stopped by the supermarket on the outskirts of Wick and picked up place mats, napkins, a set of plain wine glasses and a meal for two, easy to cook. With extra vegetables and another bottle of wine, who would tell the difference, she reasoned.

By the time she reached home, the sun was beginning its downward arc towards the west. Rays hit the windscreens of cars, a chain of sparkling diamonds tumbling down the opposite hillside.

Indoors she shivered. The old stone walls seemed to retain the cold in spite of the mild day. The feeling that the hand of fate was winding her in, bringing her back full circle persisted, and the promise she made to her father had cemented the trap. Her main fear was that after life in the city, Berriedale would be unbearably lonely and bleak in the winter. Perhaps they could sell this place, get somewhere nearer town, but given the number of for-sale signs she had seen on the way north, she doubted if that would be possible any time soon. Then there was Andy. She knew what his reaction to her decision would be.

Forget your father. He never cared for you. I'm the one who has always been here.

A finger of guilt stabbed her, yet strangely enough, she felt a sense of relief to have a valid reason not to stay in Edinburgh. What was the matter with her? They'd made a good living over the years, and she was good at her job. The club *had* been her dream too, hadn't it? Suddenly she wasn't too sure. It had been all too easy to let Andy make the decisions, to convince her that he knew what was best for her, to somehow repay him for the wrongs of the past. Yet being here, in this place, the place she once saw as a prison, she felt a sense of freedom that she had not experienced in a long time.

She pulled the Formica-topped table from the kitchen and set it up in the living room. Covered by a tablecloth and the place-mats, with a candle in the middle, it looked pretty good. After following the instructions on the packaging of the meal for two and putting it in the oven, she had time to tie her hair up and change her jeans and loose jumper for a slim-line skirt and pale green blouse. She used the straighteners on her springing hair and with a trembling hand, she applied some foundation and a slight touch of blusher. She never went in for heavy make-up.

James arrived promptly at seven carrying a bottle of wine and a bunch of flowers. He was dressed in a tweed jacket, grey flannels and an open-necked shirt, and her heart gave a slight jump when she saw him. Smiling a welcome, she led him indoors. She went to the kitchen to get a bottle of wine and when she returned he was reading the poem she had inadvertently left on the sideboard. He looked up as she entered. 'This is damn good,' he said.

'I have more editing to do,' she reached forward and snatched it from his hand.

'You wrote it? Have you any more?'

She swallowed. 'Yes. I love poetry. I used to write songs, but they fell from favour. The first couple of recordings I made were my own. After that they made me sing stuff I didn't even like because it was 'a popular style'. Anyway, I find I can say much more with free verse.' She stopped, afraid of getting carried away by her own enthusiasm.

'Is that why you gave up singing?'

'No!' Her reply was sharp.

A look of concern crossed his face. Then as if he realised he'd hit a nerve, he changed the subject. 'I read a lot of poets, old and contemporary. And, believe me, this is good.' He indicated the page now lying beside her plate. 'Have you ever thought of having them published?'

'They're very personal, but,' she lowered her eyes, debating whether to confide, then, coming to a decision, said, 'I do have them published, but not under my own name. Now come on, the food's near ready.' Andy merely tolerated her passion for poetry, seeing it as a harmless pastime. She never told him about the publishing. He would not have understood. The payments were poor.

'What name? Maybe I've heard of you.'

She hesitated, then thought, what the hell. 'Clara Spears.' She cleared her throat.

'No! Really? God, you've only been hailed as the UK's answer to Sylvia Plath.'

Beth felt the heat climb into her face. 'I wanted to be published because of my talent, not because I was well-known. That's why I originally used an pseudonym. Now I like it this way. I don't want people to know who I am.' She grinned. *You* may feel honoured.'

James drew a finger across his lips in a gesture of silence. 'But one thing I've been wondering...'

She looked at him.

'Why don't you sing any more?'

'It's no secret. I had polyps on my vocal chords. I opted for an operation, which the surgeon botched. It was in all the papers at the time.'

'I would have been overseas then. But medicine has moved on, maybe nowadays...'

'No! I've learned to live with it.'

She lifted her fork and began to eat. No, she would not risk further operations, further disappointments. 'Which poets do you read?' She changed the direction of the conversation.

He smiled, leaned towards her and said,

> *'Tis time the heart should be unmoved,*
> *Since others it hath ceased to move:*
> *Yet, though I cannot be beloved,*
> *Still let me love!*

She laughed and replied,

'My days are in the yellow leaf;
The flowers and fruits of love are gone;
The worm, the canker, and the grief
Are mine alone!'

'You like Byron?' he asked.

'Very much. Contemporary poems are fine, but they can't compare. Actually, my favourite will always be Robert Burns. Mind you, I hardly understand a lot of the words in the old Scots now. It's a pity our language is dying.'

Throughout the meal, they discussed poetry and the poets they liked, finding their tastes in literature were remarkably similar.

Setting his fork and knife to one side, James complimented her on the meal. She smiled, neither confirming nor denying the fact that she had not cooked it herself. 'It's only a steak pie,' she murmured, lowering her gaze.

A brief memory crossed her mind. A memory of a time when a neighbour brought herself and her father a casserole dish of stewed beef and it had been so good she'd eaten most of it herself. Knowing the neighbour would ask Robbie later how he enjoyed the stew, Beth opened a tin of dog food and mixed it in with the remaining gravy. She watched, as he tasted it, watched his face screw up slightly, watched him nod, watched him finish the plateful.

'Maybe not her best effort,' he said, pushing the empty dish aside.

Beth was still grinning as she returned from taking the plates to the kitchen.

'I'm sorry my mother wasn't much help.' James refilled her glass.

'At least I found out that I wasn't born around here.' She sipped her wine slowly. The first glass had made her mellow and she suddenly wished she had the means to play some background music.

'Did your parents never speak about themselves?' James said.

She shook her head. 'I asked my father once how they met.' She paused, remembering the flush of pleasure to have his attention. 'He'd had a good day at the lamb sales and a few drams before he came home, just enough to relax him.' She laughed at the memory. 'He came in, tripped over the dog, and ended up in the corner. He was all hunched up, looking at me, all guilty, as if he was a little boy and I was the mother.' She giggled. 'It was funny and we both ended up laughing. He didn't drink much.' Her voice trailed away and she became solemn. 'Now and again, when he was in that mood, I managed to get some information from him, but talking about my mother always seemed painful, even after all that time.' She fingered the stem of her glass and stared at the wall, as if she could see her life being played out there.

'They met in Bradford. They were both in the forces. He was demobbed, shrapnel in the hip. He walked with a limp afterwards. He never spoke about the war, but he had times when he would go into a mood for days.' Beth stopped and stared into the remains of the wine in her glass. 'I never wanted children. Was afraid. Afraid I wouldn't be able to cope and leave like my mother, or maybe... become disinterested like my father.'

'And you never married?'

She shook her head. 'Andy wanted to marry me and I even thought I loved him once, well, as much as I could love anyone, I guess. Maybe it was just gratitude. He took charge of the club, so I didn't have to worry, he said. What about you?'

'Been married twice. Didn't work out either time.'

'Children?'

'Two by my second wife. Boy and a girl. She took them away. They're grown up now. They keep in touch, but we're not close.'

'I'm sorry.'

'She met a guy from the States when the U.S. naval base was in Forss, up Thurso end, early warning systems in case someone in the Soviet Union got itchy fingers. I was doing my first stint in Africa. When the Russian threat was removed and the Americans went home, she left with him. Took the kids. I couldn't really blame her, me leaving her alone for so long must have been hard. I went to Colorado to see the children once, but it was awkward. They look on their stepfather as their real dad.'

'I vaguely remember the base. Do you keep in touch with your kids?'

'Yes, but only via Facebook. Beth, why have you left it till now to find out about your past?'

'I always meant to try one day, but life was pretty hectic. There just wasn't the time.' She could not admit she was scared she'd be rejected again. She didn't want to face the fact that Andy's words fuelled her fear. 'My father's illness has forced me to realise, that if I don't do it soon, I'll die without ever knowing the truth.' She turned to face James. 'Seeing him. I thought... what if the same thing happens to me... and I'm lying trapped inside my mind never knowing. I'm so glad you traced me.' She laughed, embarrassed at her uncharacteristic openness. 'I don't know why I'm telling you all this. I hardly know you.'

'It's the best way, isn't it?'

'No, I should stop. Andy's always said it's best to let sleeping dogs lie.'

'I don't think you should. God willing, we'll have another twenty, thirty years of active life ahead of us. After all, sixty's the new forty.' He was watching her, his eyes kind. 'But you've got to lay the ghosts.'

Beth stared into the ruby depths of her wine. 'There was one time which sticks in my mind.'

'Go on.'

'It was summer, but Dad made me wear wellington boots. I hadn't wanted to put them on at first. I can still hear my father's words. "We're going through deep heather and you might disturb an adder," I remember him standing there, all brown and healthy looking. He was lean, he was always very lean. He was a handsome man. After that I didn't complain. I didn't relish being bitten by

63

a snake.' A little smile played around her mouth. She cleared her throat. 'And then I saw an eagle in the distance. I remember clinging to Dad's leg. I was afraid even then.

"Damn birds," Dad swore. "Vermin, that's what they are. Killing all the game. How is the estate going to make money if there's no game left for the hunters?"

'I started to cry and he picked me up. "He might think you're a wee lamb and steal you away. I couldn't stand it if I lost you too." And he hugged me. I remember it especially because at that moment, I felt he would keep me safe.'

James reached over and covered her hand with his.

She enjoyed the feel of his skin next to hers. 'Could be why I've always been afraid of eagles,' she said.

'You're afraid of eagles? How afraid?'

'Very. A phobia. All big birds in fact.'

'In that case, I think it would be something much more dramatic.'

James squeezed her hand, his eyes never leaving her face.

For a brief moment she wondered how he would react if she asked him to stay the night. Twenty years ago, he would have asked her already, she reflected, amused at her own thoughts. How long had it been since a man had affected her like this? A brief memory of Lewis Hammond and how that affair almost destroyed her rose unbidden. Just as quickly, she banished it back into the folder in her head filed under "mistakes best forgotten." Suddenly uneasy, she withdrew her hand from his and glanced at the clock. 'I'll need to get to bed soon. I'm going to drive to Inverness tomorrow and I want an early start.'

'You're not sending me away already? I haven't unburdened *my* soul yet.' He lifted his brows as if in a question.

'Okay, another....,' she checked the last bottle of wine. It was half-full. 'Another drink, then you really have to go.'

His long fingers played with the stem of his glass. 'Didn't you ever want to find your mother?'

'For years I dreamed I'd bump into her in the street and we'd immediately recognise each other. But all my childhood, she could've come back if she'd wanted me.' Her voice carried a raw edge now. 'I tried to blot it out, tried to pretend I had no family. That I needed no one.'

'Maybe she tried to get in touch when she sorted her life. How would she know where you lived after you left? You told me your father didn't even know.'

'I suppose you're right.' She stared at his hand, at the fingers on the stem of his glass, the short clean nails, imagined them on her skin, and immediately lifted her eyes. 'But he knew later, when I sent him my address. He didn't reply, not once!' She gave a deep sigh. 'It's too late for regrets. It's doubtful if she's still alive.' But his words had the effect of cracking a shell, allowing some of the raw emotion to leak out. With all the effort she possessed, she closed the shell and sealed the edges. What was the matter with her? She was talking too much. Wanting too much. She drained her glass and looked at the clock.

'I've enjoyed myself tonight,' James said, standing up. 'Look, if the weather stays fine, how about you and I taking a hike up to Eagle Rock some day?'

'No!' the word exploded before she could stop it. 'No, I can't.'

He looked confused. 'I'm sorry, did I say something wrong?'

'No, it's just, well, I told you about me and birds.'

'I doubt if they'll come near us. It's just the name of a place. It's where the Duke of Kent's plane crashed in WW2.'

'I know.' How could she tell him that even the word 'eagle' filled her with an irrational fear? 'But you're right. I'm being silly.' She suddenly couldn't wait to get him out of the door, get it shut and bolted.

'Then we'll go?' He looked concerned.

'Yes, we will.' She spoke without any intentions of going up a mountain and definitely not to a place called Eagle Rock. Tomorrow would be another day. Another excuse.

'And you'll come to my place next time? I make a mean curry.' He bent down and kissed her cheek and the warmth of his lips lingered. 'And I want to read more of your poems.'

'Yes, I'll do that.' She moved away, trying not to meet his eyes. 'Goodnight.'

She closed the door and hugged herself, simultaneously missing his presence and glad to be alone. She almost opened up to him tonight. Draining what was left of the wine she leaned back in the chair.

She would never find sleep now. Once more her thoughts moved to her father.

Looking back from her adult eyes, she realised how difficult it must have been for him. She, as a moody, sulky child, hadn't been easy. Then she hit her teens and was filled with angst and anger. If only he had spoken to her more, they might have been close. How could she have understood his reasons, his rage? How could she have made things different?

Her mind carried her back to the day she discovered both the seed of rebellion that had been germinating in her soul, and her love of singing.

Chapter Six

The day began like any other. At the bus stop she removed her boots and thick stockings. Bare legs and well-worn shoes were marginally better than roughly-knitted socks and well-worn shoes. They would still draw jeers and sniggers of course. She shrunk against the wall of the shelter as the other children filed in. Girls grouped together and laughed. Largely they ignored her, sometimes they looked her way and tittered. She turned her eyes to the sky and pretended she didn't care, that she didn't want someone to speak to her, show her some act of kindness, that she didn't desperately want to be part of the crowd. She hated being the odd girl with jug ears who sang to herself and wore hand-me-down clothes.

Miss Thomson, the music teacher, had asked for anyone who wanted to sing in the upcoming festival to come to her room after school for an audition.

Singing was the one thing Beth loved, the one thing which lifted her from her life and made her heart soar. Her father would not be home until seven o'clock anyway, so there was nothing to stop her from staying behind.

'I'm so glad you came along, Elizabeth,' said Miss Thomson when she saw her. 'I've heard you sing in class. This audition will be a walk in the park for you.' Miss Thomson was nice; she was young and slim and smelt of flowers. Afterwards, as Beth left the building, a boy who had also been auditioning, a boy she knew as Magnus, ran up behind her. 'Wait a minute,' he shouted.

Unused to talking to boys, her face reddened.

'You're a really good singer,' he said.

And time stood still. She smiled. Knowing she was.

'The best there today,' he continued.

'Not better than you.'

'Different. Why don't you come and sing with our group? We're meeting up at the hall on Friday night.

'I'd love to,' she said. At the same time panicking because she had nothing to wear. But knowing she had to do this.

On Friday night, she washed and ironed her hair and dressed in her jeans and a blouse which she thought looked half-way decent.

'I've made scrambled eggs,' she said when her father returned from the fields. 'You can heat them up. I'm going out.'

He raised his eyes and looked at her as if he'd never seen her before. 'Going out where?' he asked, an edge in his voice.

'I've been asked to sing with a group.'

'Boys?'

'Yeees, I suppose.' She fisted her hair and pressed her knees together to stop the tremble. She wanted this more than she wanted anything, except, perhaps, her mother to return.

Robbie's face grew red. 'No,' he shouted, banging his fist on the table, making her jump. He had never raised his voice to her before, ever.

'But why?' Her scalp prickled.

'I know what boys are like. You're too young.'

She felt her anger bubble up. She never asked for anything from him. 'I'm only going to sing. Please, I want to.'

He levelled his finger at her. 'Whores and comic singers. You start going out, drinking, getting up to who knows what, next you'll be leaving, just like your mother.'

It was the first time in her memory that he'd mentioned her mother without prompting. Suddenly singing with the group was far from her mind. 'Why did she leave, Dad?' Beth pulled in her chair. Talk to me, she pleaded silently. Please tell me what happened. She would have stayed here with him, forgotten the band, if only he had opened up and told her what she wanted to know.

'You will not sing with a band and you will not leave this house tonight.' He rose quickly, the chair falling to the ground behind him and clattering on the floor. With a final glare at her he stormed over to the cooker and lifted the lid from the pan. With his voice suddenly calm again, he said, 'Eggs look good.'

'Please, Dad, I want to know about my mam.'

He turned. 'Your mother's dead to us. I never want to hear her name mentioned in this house again, understand?'

'But I need to know...'

She was rewarded by the turn of his back.

Damn him, she thought, years of frustration welling up inside her, threatening to explode. 'I'm going to my room,' she shouted. 'And I don't want to speak to you ever again.' She ran upstairs and slammed the door.

Pans and plates rattled downstairs as he heated up the eggs, his anger making his movements fast and clumsy.

'Are you coming down for your dinner?' he called after a while.

'No,' she screamed, kicking the door.

She eased her window open and looked at the ground one storey below. She had to go tonight. If she didn't they might not ask again. She wondered if the tree outside her window would be strong enough to bear her weight and decided it wasn't.

'Have you fed the hens?' Robbie was shouting again.

Wordlessly she marched down the stairs, went to the back porch and got the feed bucket. The chickens had been fed, but she wouldn't tell him that. Slamming doors and stamping her feet, she went outside and round the back of the house. From the barn she dragged out several packing cases, which were used to shelter new lambs in the spring, and built one on top of the other, testing them for safety as she went along. If she climbed out of her window and lowered herself as far as she could, her feet should touch the top box.

She went back indoors.

'Are you going to eat something?' said her father.

'No,' she screamed at him.

'Then the dog'll get it.'

'Fine by me.'

She slammed her bedroom door and turned her transistor up as loud as it would go. Once more she opened the window and this time climbed out, carefully lowering herself onto the boxes, jumping from one to the other before the top one wobbled and fell. She hit the

71

ground and stood still, listening for her father's roar as he came round the corner. It never happened. She wasn't afraid he would hit her, he never had, but then she had never defied him before.

Backstage she froze. Sorry,' she said. 'I shouldn't have come. I can't go out there.' She closed and opened her fists. What had she been thinking? She was dressed like a tramp and looked like a monkey, she would make a fool of herself and everyone would laugh at her. She felt physically sick.

Magnus opened a large coke bottle and handed it to her. 'Have a drink, it'll calm you.'

'Coke?' She screwed up her face.

The others laughed.

'With a wee bit o' Dutch courage added,' Magnus thrust it at her.

She put the bottle to her lips and drank. It burned all the way down, and it seemed there was very little coke in it. She drank again, forcing the liquid past her throat which tried to close in protest.

'Hey, leave some for the rest of us.' Magnus took the bottle from her. 'That's my dad's best vodka in there.'

Unaccustomed to strong liquor, Beth had already stopped shaking. By the time they were due to go on stage she was stepping on air, the room spun and she could have sung for the queen.

That was the beginning. Once she started to sing she forgot her father's wrath, forgot her big ears, forgot everything except that it was her turn to shine. By the time her song ended, tears were streaming down her face.

There were many such nights after that, and as her love of singing grew, so did her father's anger, until the cold atmosphere which dwelt within the house, became hostile and restrictive.

Chapter Seven

Early next morning, Beth opened her eyes with a start, a dream already fading from her mind, yet leaving a sensation of dread. Stretching, glad she had power back in her limbs, she waited as the memories of the night fractured and dissolved. The Venetian blinds rattled. A frisson of fear caught her breath. The window had blown open sometime during the night, yet she felt sure she checked it before she went to bed. But she couldn't have, that was it, she was growing forgetful, she told herself.

She rose, padded to the window and pulled it shut. Clouds raced across a blue sky, throwing fast-moving shadows up the strath. The pale snake of a road wound before her, a lorry almost doubling back on itself to negotiate the hairpin bend. On the opposite hill she could make out James' house, its white walls catching the morning sun, glinting through the trees. She turned her eyes towards the sea, an undulating grey-blue plane, and further out still, the faded solidity of oil rigs. She closed her eyes and allowed her breathing to slow down. There was something wrong with the window catches, that was all, she told herself.

James arrived early with a toolbox. 'I've come to fix your windows,' he said. 'Is that coffee I can smell?'

'Of course,' she led him indoors, clutching her dressing gown at her throat. It was almost ten o'clock, but he did not seemed the least perturbed by finding her still in her night clothes. Self-consciously, she ran a hand through her hair. After filling the kettle, she spooned instant coffee into two mugs. James had already begun to check the catch on the kitchen window.

'They seem fine,' he said, frowning slightly.

'Then could you put locks on them?'

'On them all?'

'Yes. Every window in the house.' She clutched her mug tightly in an attempt to stop her hands from shaking. The fact that there was nothing wrong with the catches scared her more than her dreams. *Had she opened them herself? Was it happening again? The forgetfulness? The way it happened after she came back from London? The confusion which had made her so dependent on Andy? No. She was stronger now and she didn't need him. She really didn't. Yet the memory of his voice remained in her head.* 'You can't cope on your own, Beth. You need me.'

'Are you okay?' James was looking at her, concern in his eyes.

She tightened her fingers and nodded quickly.

'It's possible the frame moves with the wind and the catch comes loose that way. Locks are a good idea,' he said. 'Ideally, you should replace these windows.'

'I might not be staying very long.' She thought of Andy. Compared his reaction.

'For God's sake, Beth, you must have done it. There's no one else here except you and me, and I sure as hell didn't. I'll have to watch you more closely, that's all.'

As James fitted the locks, she bathed and dressed. With her damp hair knotted at the back of her head, she rubbed a layer of cream into her skin and added a touch of colour to her cheeks. She was always too pale. Back in the kitchen, the kettle was making the rushing noise that precedes boiling.

'All done,' said James. 'Ready for another coffee?'

'Please,' she replied.

'Have you ever spoken to anyone, a professional?' he asked as they sat across the table from one another.

'You mean like a shrink? About what?' Her fingers tightened around her cup.

'You're fear of birds for one thing, your inability to remember the past for another.'

'I did once.'

'Did it help you to remember?'

She shrugged, suddenly uncomfortable. 'The therapist explained a lot of things which made sense at the time. But then, well,' Beth stared at her cup, 'I felt I didn't need her any more.'

'You stopped it?'

'Yes, I stopped it.' Had she? Andy was the one who thought it was doing more harm than good and she was more than happy to leave at the time. The probing questions were beginning to disturb her.

'Would you consider going back?'

'Why?'

'Talking helps. Trust me, I have experience in that field.'

'Well, I'm talking to you aren't I? Why won't you do?'

'Although I *have* studied psychology, my area of expertise is the body, not the mind.'

'You're easy to talk to.' Too easy, she thought. She rose and walked over to the sink where she rinsed out her cup.

'Are you afraid to remember?'

'Maybe.' She remained quiet for a long minute, then came to a decision. 'But I do want to find out what happened to Michael. And the nightmares, they never quite went away. When I buried myself in my career I could cope, but when I lost that... I did drink a lot, I may as well be honest. Tried different drugs too, but I was never addicted.' She didn't add, although Andy tried to convince me I was.

'Nightmares?'

'Periodically it happens. Ever since I was a child. Coming back here... ' she shrugged. 'I dream about eagles. Scary dreams.' She gave an embarrassed laugh. 'There must be a reason for it, mustn't there?'

'I would say so. Look, let's start at the beginning. Have you got your birth certificate? It should mention where you were born.'

'Couldn't find it in my father's box of memories.'

'Then we'll do a search. Order the original. We can do that online. And if we start with your parents we should be able to find out if they had another child.'

'We?'

'You've got me curious, too. Have you got a computer?'

'Not with me.'

'Then let's go to mine.'

She looked at her watch. 'I can't spend too much time just now, I have shopping to do.'

77

'You know what, I'm impatient. I don't want to wait for a copy. Are you going to town?'

'That was the plan.'

'Come on then. Bring all your details and your parents' marriage certificate.'

'What are you planning?' she asked as they drove along the road to Wick.

'The registrar's office. We know when your parents were married, you know when you were born, they'll be able to do a search and issue the documents there and then, no need to wait for the post.'

The registrar was an obliging lady of undetermined age. After James explained what they needed, she smiled. 'I'm sure I can help you,' she said and took a seat in front of the computer.

She leaned towards the screen for what Beth felt was a long time, then her face lit up. 'I've found your brother,' she said.

'What?' Beth forgot to breathe.

'Michael Robert MacLean, born 2nd October 1947 in Inverness.' She looked at Beth over the rim of her glasses. 'I assume you want a copy?'

Beth bobbed her head. 'And his death, when did he die?'

The printer whirred to life and made a humming noise before spitting out a sheet of paper. Beth moistened her lips. She wished she was close enough to snatch it.

The registrar's finger tapped quickly, she negotiated the mouse. After a series of clicks, her face relaxed again. 'He died on the 29th September 1959. Cause of death, multiple injuries. They were living in Fort William by then. Father's profession, gamekeeper.'

Beth grew hot as if her blood were on fire. It doesn't make sense. Nettie said my mother was a city girl. Fort William is hardly a city.'

Once again the printer clicked and another sheet of paper whooshed on top of the last.

'And yours of course.' More taps and clicks and whirrs and a third sheet joined the others.

'Let me see.' She took the copies with a shaking hand and stared at the proof of Michael's existence. 'God, he was only twelve years old,' she whispered. 'Multiple injuries, what does that mean?'

James removed his wallet from his jacket pocket and paid for the certificates.

'I was born in Inverness, too,' she said, looking at her own certificate. 'Here, I'll pay for them.'

'Not at all.' James took Beth's arm. 'We'll get the shopping, then while you're putting them away, I'll go home and begin supper. I'll take care of these for now.' He removed the papers from her hand and slipped them into a brown envelope which the registrar had handed to him. 'I'll take care of them until later. We'll discuss the next move over food and wine.'

She hesitated for a moment, then nodded. 'You drive, I don't think I'd be safe on the road right now.'

Chapter Eight

'Beth, for God's sake will you answer my calls.' Andy pushed his mobile into his pocket, exasperated after once more being directed to her voice mail. 'I'm taking some time off,' he said to the man carrying a guitar case into the pub.

'You can't,' said Bill. 'Both of you can't be gone at the same time. We've had a cancellation for the weekend, who's going to fill in?' Bill was a member of the resident band, in which Andy also played lead guitar.

'I'm worried about Beth.'

'For heaven's sake, man, she's a grown woman. What good can you do?'

Andy ran his fingers over the stubble of what was left of his hair. 'Good God, how can you say that, Bill? You know the problems I've had with her in the past.'

Bill's face grew red. 'She's a damn hard grafter. You should have a replacement band for Saturday night. We've been playing all week. I promised Muriel to take her out for a meal.'

'I'll pay you extra.'

'The punters come for something special at the weekend. If they come here and it's only us, minus our lead guitarist, they'll leave in droves. And I'll be banned from the marital bed for the foreseeable future.'

'If that's how it must be.' Andy curbed his temper. Damn the woman taking off just as their popularity was hitting an all-time high. He'd been wrong to let her go at all. He went into his office and sat down, his head in his hands. It had been Beth who arranged all the bookings.

What the hell was she thinking, charging up to Caithness without arranging an act for this weekend? Her father had not been in her life since she was sixteen, for God's sake.

Andy only agreed to her leaving for a couple of days, and only because she'd been so distressed after the phone call. He didn't think she would be much use to him in that state anyway. If he'd answered the phone himself she would never have known. He sucked air through his teeth. The fear she might not return had been plaguing him ever since.

The first time she'd left him was in 1982. They'd managed to get a gig as a supporting act for the Alexander Brothers, and, what really excited both of them, there was a talent scout in the area. Rumour had it he would be in the audience that night. What Andy didn't know then was that the scout would love Beth's voice, and he would only want her.

Andy was fool enough to expect loyalty, but the promise of stardom had been too great a pull for a young wannabe star. It was more than that. Hammond was smooth and handsome and sophisticated, and he had enough money to sweep Beth off her feet. At first she was reluctant to take up the offer without her friends, and they'd discussed it all night. Andy could see the excitement in her eyes, understand how much she really wanted this.

In his mind's eye, Andy saw her again, rushing around the bedroom opening drawers and doors, throwing her things into a hold-all.

81

'This is a mistake,' he said.

She stopped and looked at him, a dress hanging from her hand. 'I can't believe you want me to give up this chance.' There was accusation in her eyes. 'It's not as if I'll be gone forever. And if this works out, I'll see you get your chance as well. I've already told you. I'll be in the know, then, Andy.' She never looked lovelier. Her riot of soft red curls danced round her head as she moved. Her grey-green eyes sparkled. 'Once I've made it, I'll demand that you and Desmond come and be my backing band.' She came over and took his hand. 'Please don't make this hard.'

But she had not kept her promise. She went away and forgot him – just as she was going to do now.

Chapter Nine.

Beth went upstairs and made a start on her old bedroom. She stripped off the bedding and upended the mattress, only to find a hole in the bottom. No doubt mice had made a home there over the years. She dragged it outside and abandoned it a little way from the house. She would phone the Highland Council to collect it later. Back inside, she vacuumed away the dust of the years, packed the bedding in a plastic bag and relegated it to the bin. Once the room was clean and fresh, she took her car into Wick, where she bought a large tin of emulsion paint, a duvet, a complete set of bedding and curtains. She was delighted to find a memory-foam mattress was rolled up so tightly it would fit into her car. She did some food shopping and ate lunch in a small cafe in the centre of town. That done, she drove home, pleased with her day's purchases.

By the time she stood on James' doorstep, day had slipped from the sky, leaving a black dome and a full moon.

'Come in, come in,' he immediately stepped back to allow her to enter. The kitchen smelled pleasantly of spices. He led her to the dining room where the table was set tastefully for two.

'It's nice,' she said, looking at the white tablecloth set with red and white place mats and a red candle in the middle.

He pulled out her chair and waited until she was seated before speaking. 'We'll go to the address in Fort William. Talk to people, do a search on the backdated local newspapers, find out what happened. We could leave tomorrow morning, drop in to see your father on the way then stay overnight in the Fort. What do you think?'

'I'm not sure.' Her hand flew to her throat. Now, faced with the possibility of finding out the truth, a fear gripped her.

He took a bottle of wine from the rack and poured her a drink. 'Dinner'll be ready in five minutes. He covered her hand with his. 'Don't worry. I'll be with you.'

'I don't know. Maybe...' She stared into her glass.

'Tell me the truth. Will you ever be at peace if you back out now?'

In spite of the sudden sensation that once again a man was telling her what to do, organising her life, Beth cleared her throat and shook her head. 'No. And I wish I'd done it sooner.' She took a deep breath. 'But you really shouldn't have done this. I'm sorry if I come across as a needy female, it was just that coming back here threw me. I am capable of sorting out my life on my own.'

He drew back as if stung. 'I'm sorry if I sounded patronising, I really didn't mean... look, you'd do me a favour by letting me come with you. Life has begun to get boring lately.' He raised his eyebrows slightly and she couldn't help laughing at his little-boy-chastised expression.

She did want his help, want his support. 'Alright, if that's the only reason. I'm sorry if I sounded sharp. Let's do it.' She tightened her fingers around his.

'Good.' He nodded. 'Now come and sit at the table.'

After the meal, which was surprisingly good, they sat together before a roaring fire. 'You're very quiet. Still worried?' he asked.

She stared into the flames and twisted her glass around. 'It's a shock. I had a brother who died. A brother my parents never told me about.' But, she thought, what if the truth was something terrible? She lifted her eyes to his. He leant towards her so she could smell the wine on his breath.

She set her glass on the table. 'James.'

He put down his own drink. 'Hush,' he said.

It came over her suddenly. She wanted more than anything to kiss him at this moment. She had never felt like this for years, had thought herself past all that, and the strength of her longing frightened her.

His lips barely brushed hers and her arms snaked around his neck. He pulled away, at the same time his hands gripped her wrists. 'Are you sure this is what you want?'

'Yes,' she whispered. At this moment she was very sure.

'I can't,' he said.

'The force of her longing was suddenly replaced by the heat of embarrassment. She jerked herself away from him, clutching her hands to her chest. 'I'm...sorry, I read the signs wrong... I'm sorry.' She turned her flaming face away from him and rose. 'I'll go...go now.' She stumbled

85

to the door, but he was there before her, his arm blocking her way.

'The signs weren't wrong,' he said. 'I find you very attractive, but if I were to take advantage of the situation, it would be just that... taking advantage. You're vulnerable, and I'm not sure of your motives. I don't want to risk spoiling what's happening between us.' He turned her round to face him.

'I am not that vulnerable. I know what I want.' God, how did she sound? Like she was a tart? She lowered her head. He put his hand beneath her chin and lifted her face so she looked directly at him.

'There's nothing I would like more,' he whispered, 'Than to spend the night with you, but right now it would be wrong. If anything ever happens between us, it has to be for the right reasons.'

She studied him for a while, trying to decide whether this was his way of letting her down gently, or if he really was being honest. The only thing she was sure of at this moment, was that she'd made a fool of herself. She should have waited, let him make the first move, if there was to be any.

'I'd better go then,' she said, and turned towards the door.

'I'll walk you home.' He set a hand on her shoulder.

No, the moon's bright. I'll be fine. Goodnight.' She pulled away, not too quickly.

'Don't be daft. I'm coming with you. No argument.'

They walked together in silence. Once they reached her front door, she turned to him. 'Thank you,' she said, her voice low.

He bent towards her, his lips briefly touching her cheek. 'See you tomorrow,' he whispered and squeezed her arm. She unlocked the door, slipped inside and stood behind it with her eyes shut. 'Fool, fool, fool,' she whispered to no one.

Chapter Ten

That night she lay in her own bed in the room where she slept as a child, unable to find peace. With no desire to dwell on James' rejection, she diverted her mind down the years, no longer fighting memories. She realised in these last few hours that what she wanted more than anything at this time, was to find the truth, find out what was behind the locked door in her mind, the place she was afraid to go. What was her earliest recollection? It was patchy, but it came at her in bits and pieces.

She had been lying in this same bed, listening to the sounds of raised voices. The woman was crying. 'I closed my eyes for a moment, only a moment.' The words were an echo, over and over again. Terror had held Beth in its grip. A dark shadow hung over the house back then, infiltrating every corner, filling her bedroom, making it difficult for her to breathe. And somehow, she imagined it was all her fault.

The memory passed. A flash, a mere glimpse of the past, fading as quickly as it came. Finally, she drifted away on the soft cloud of sleep and her dreams took her to another place.

She was on a mountainside. Not the slow rising mountains outside her door, but a high, rugged mountain with steep, jagged cliffs, a waterfall gushing a little way off, the thunder of it filling her ears. And someone was with her, someone with a blank face. She was calling to the figure but her voice was silent. Then he turned and there was a mouth in the blank face and it opened and as it opened the figure tripped and pitched forward and Beth watched it sail through the air, bouncing slowly from ledge to ledge, arms and legs splayed. There was only one scream, long and drawn out, and that scream echoed from hill to hill and the echo remained after the figure disappeared under the water in the gorge below.

Beth was aware it was a dream and forced herself to wake up. Lying in the semi-blackness, listening to the silence broken only by the tick of a clock, she heard another scream and she knew it was the scream of an eagle.

Sweat dampened her skin, the duvet lay in a tangle. She tried to lift her hand but movement was impossible, her legs and arms were stiff, her body cemented onto the bed. She felt herself being dragged back into a yawning dark well of murkiness where she knew the eagle waited.

There was a rustle at the window and it blew open. The eagle would be there. He had come for her because she'd been with Michael. Michael! She woke then, really woke, with the name on her lips and the room was still dark, the deep darkness which comes with moonless nights before the first whisper of dawn. She covered her head with the sheet.

The next time she opened her eyes, a thin shaft of sunshine filtered in where the curtains didn't quite meet and, fully awake, she realised the screaming had been inside her head. The thought of going to Fort William, confronting her past, had been responsible for the nightmare, she decided. She considered changing her mind. The curtains fluttered and a cool breeze caressed her face. She shot upright. The window was open. She was sure she'd locked it last night. But had she? She'd been upset, drunk maybe a few wines too many. Yes, that must be it, it must be, she convinced herself.

She rose, bathed and dressed slowly, trying to recapture the dream which faded like smoke on the wind leaving only faint wisps flirting around the edge of her consciousness.

A cup of coffee and two painkillers later, she heard the throb of an engine followed by the crunch of wheels on the drive as a vehicle drew up outside. She crossed to the window, expecting to see James' car, but a familiar Audi was parked in front and alighting from it was the last person she wanted to see at this moment. With a resigned sigh, she opened the front door.

'Andy, what are you doing here?'

'I was worried about you.' He closed the car door carefully behind him. He was immaculately dressed as usual and looking every inch the successful businessman. His fitness regime kept his body firm over the years, his remaining hair was shaved to give his head a modern look. 'You're not answering my calls.' His eyes flickered over the cottage exterior and his distaste showed plainly on his face. A brief memory of the fresh-faced boy from the Western Isles with the long hair, strong jaw and hippy clothes, flashed through her mind, and she wondered where he had gone.

'I told you about the reception here and there's no need to worry; I told you I was fine.'

'You didn't sound fine and you certainly don't look fine.'

'I had a restless night.' As soon as the words left her mouth, she knew it was the wrong thing to say. She turned away. 'You might as well come in. I'll put on the kettle.'

He followed her into the kitchen, gazing around, judging everything. 'It's easy for you to get down, Beth. You need me, you know you do.'

She stopped her tongue. She wanted to say, no, Andy, I do not need you. I'm managing fine. Instead she asked, 'What about the club?'

'They can get by without me for a wee while, you're more important. Glenda's keeping an eye on things. I thought we could go for a run today. I've never been to John O' Groats. We'll stop in somewhere for a meal, cheer you up.'

'Actually I planned to go to Inverness. I came here for my father, remember.'

He gave a pah of irritation. 'I've driven all night to be with you, by the way. The least you could do is spend some time with me.'

'I didn't ask you to come.' The words left her mouth before she could trap them.

His brows screwed down, the intake of breath hissed through his teeth. 'I knew how coming back here would affect you. My own fault for letting you go. You've not been well, Beth, you shouldn't be on your own. Come on, get me a coffee and then we'll talk.'

'I'm grateful, I really am... but I need to do this without you.' What was the use. He would never understand. 'Furthermore,' she added, 'I'm not all that sure Glenda can manage on her own.' Glenda had worked with them for six years now, a single girl, twice divorced, with looks which drew in the punters and eyes that coveted everything Beth owned.

'Haven't you missed me at all?' He reached for her. This time she allowed the embrace but remained tense.

'Of course. It's just that there's no need for us to lose money.'

'It's only for a couple of days. I'll come to Inverness with you. Meet your father, then we'll go home to Edinburgh. Nothing stopping you taking the train up twice a month. We'll talk about residential care. I assume that's what he's going to need.'

'No, Andy. I... I want to look after him, here, in his own home.' She cringed inside, waiting for his reaction.

'Don't be so ridiculous. What about the club? You can't expect me to sell up and move here. God, that's not what you have in mind, is it?'

'No. I don't expect you to sell up or move here.'

'What are you saying? You're leaving me, is this what you're saying? For God's sake, girl, you'll be in pieces within a month. You look after an invalid... ha, you can't even look after yourself.'

She bit her lip and dropped her eyes to the table top.

'Look, okay. If it's so important, we'll take him to Edinburgh. Find a home there. We'll give Glenda a bit more responsibility, spend more time together ...'

'That's good of you.' She cleared her throat. 'But I have to take him home... to his home, make up for all the years...'

'You mean all the years he didn't give a shite about you? All the years I've had to look after you?'

She pressed her eyes closed fighting her weakening resolve. 'I don't know for sure what I'm going to do. Please give me a bit more time. And... for now, I'm sure Glenda'll give you all the help you need.' Yes, she thought, Glenda would be only too happy to give him all the help he needed. At one time she considered getting rid of her, but right now the young woman's scheming suited her. Glenda wanted her business, she wanted Andy. Andy, she could have, but not the club.

'Then let's go back home. We'll talk about it there.'

Beth moved away from him. 'There's something else I must do. Let me do it myself, please. Then we'll talk, I promise.'

She saw the pulse beat at his temple, saw the determined press of the lips, and knew he was struggling to remain calm.

Once she'd made the coffee, they sat facing each other across the table and she told him about James and what they discovered, but nothing about the dreams and not about last night. She took a deep breath. 'I've got to find out what happened all those years ago. Maybe if I tell my father I know about Michael, tell him I'm back for him, maybe he'll die in peace.'

She watched Andy's hands tighten around his cup, watched as the jaw clenched. Waited for the outburst and cringed against the tension in the air.

He stood up quickly.

'I knew it.' His voice was low. 'I should have never let you come up here alone. More fool me.' His steel-grey

93

eyes glittered. 'Now this...this...James has encouraged you to drag everything up again. So what if you once had a brother? You've done without your family all these years and if he's dead and gone, what does it matter? It's not as if you knew him. Years I've spent helping you forget and now... now,' his face reddened. Spittle formed at the edges of his mouth. 'Forget Fort William. You're coming home with me today, now.' His desperate eyes bore into hers.

'No...no...I'm not.' Her voice wavered.

'You're better than *this, this hovel*.' He indicated round the room. 'We both are, we've moved on. Why would you want to take a step back in time?'

'I...I...,' Her voice failed her. How could she explain when she didn't know herself?

The door opened and James stood there, filling the space. Andy spun around.

'James, this is my partner, Andy,' said Beth, glad of the diversion.

Andy glared at him.

James nodded without offering a hand.

'I can't say I'm pleased to meet you,' said Andy, narrowing his eyes. 'You don't know the harm you've done. Beth can't cope with this.' He lowered his voice. 'Look, I know you mean well, but I know Beth's history. I'm taking her back home. It's where she needs to be.'

James looked past him and raised his eyebrows. 'Beth?'

Beth swallowed and there was nothing to swallow. 'I *am* home,' she said.

James looked again at Andy and shrugged his shoulders. 'It's up to her, don't you think?'

'You don't understand. If it wasn't for me she'd be in an institution. She's crazy.' Andy turned to Beth. 'Have you been taking your medication?'

She felt the blood drain from her face. James' presence gave her bravado. 'I don't need medication. I've not been taking it for months.'

'What?' Andy spluttered. 'And look what happened. You look like shite, by the way.'

'Medication is not the answer,' said James quietly.

'It's got damn all to do with you.' Andy rounded on him. 'You know bugger all about her life.'

James ignored him. 'I'll wait for you in the car.' He nodded at Beth and without looking at Andy, turned and left.

Beth wanted to scream at him to stay, to give her the strength she so badly needed right now. 'I've got to do this,' she whispered.

Andy's voice became smooth. 'You need rest, love, a holiday. I'll take you to the Maldives, you know how you've always wanted to go there. You'll forget all this, I promise you.' He walked towards her and set his hand on her arm. 'I'm never going to let you go again. Now go and pack a few things. I'll wait here.'

As Beth folded her clothes and set them in the suitcase, her mind was in turmoil. Was Andy right? Would finding out what happened do more harm than good? She had been tempted to back out even before Andy's visit, and where was the strength to defy him? She closed the case, looped her jacket over her arm, took a long look around the room, and walked into the living area.

'I'm not coming with you, Andy.' She was amazed at words she had not planned, and the sense of relief that saying them gave her.

She watched surprise bleed from his eyes and turn to disbelief. 'You can't cope without me,' he spluttered. 'I love you too much to let it all happen again. Now stop being so stupid. '

'I'm not going with you,' she repeated, stronger. 'You might be right. This might be a bad idea, but I've got to do it. Otherwise I'll never find peace.'

'But...Beth, please...' He stared at her as if he'd never seen her before. His voice became desperate. 'You can't mean this? I'll even take your father to live with us, get a nurse, what else do you want me to do?'

She set her hand on his arm. 'Forgive me, but my mind's made up.'

'Look, I'll take you to Fort William. I'll do anything ...' He grabbed her arm. 'Please, love, don't leave me.'

'Just let me go, Andy.'

He dropped his hand and his face darkened. 'I never thought you'd leave me again for another man, not after what happened last time.'

'For goodness sake, that was completely different, and there's nothing but friendship between me and James. Please let me do this. I've got to find out, can't you see that?'

'All I can see is him. He's wanting more than friendship.'

'Don't be ridiculous. I'm not going to stand here and argue with you. Goodbye Andy. I've got to lock up.'

He shook his head. She thought she saw tears in his eyes. Surprised, she almost laughed. 'Go now,' she said, turning away.

He said no more as he left, his shoulders slumped, his hands dangling by his sides.

'How do you feel?' asked James as they sped along the road.

'I feel free.' Overcome with a swelling in her heart, she threw her head back and laughed. She just realised she really did.

Once she became serious, she studied the profile of the man beside her. His strong jaw, his chiselled nose. 'James,' she said, 'I haven't asked before, but I need to know about my father.'

James took a breath. 'There's not much to tell. From what I know, he had been suffering clinical depression for many years, but refused to acknowledge it. He spoke about you often. He was very proud, you know.'

'When he didn't answer my letter, I thought he hadn't forgiven me, that he'd shut the door.'

'No. He retreated into his own world, became a recluse. He believed you were better off without him.'

'Montgomery should have contacted me anyway. I would have come home if I'd known.'

'He couldn't go against a patient's wishes.'

Silence fell within the car.

Chapter Eleven.

They drove into Fort William, a town of which she had no recollection. The streets were thronged with tourists even though it was late in the year. With the help of the sat-nav, they found the address easily. A small cottage on the outskirts, in the shadow of Ben Nevis. From the outside it looked bright and clean with a rear extension that spoke of recent renovation. She studied the quaint building and the garden, trying to find something familiar, some sense of recognition. Something made her shiver, either the sharp wind which swept up the glen or something completely different.

James didn't speak, but squeezed her arm gently as they walked up the path. When they stood in front of the door, a deep green door with a bevelled glass panel and a brass knocker in the shape of a lion's head with a ring in its mouth, one hand reached out to grasp James', the other rose, reached towards the knocker, stopped, remained suspended for a moment. She gave James a tight smile to indicate she was fine, cleared her throat and rapped three times. There was no answer. She stepped back and looked at the windows, wondering which had been her bedroom. She rapped again and listened to the echoing silence.

'Seems like no one's home,' said James. We can always come back later. Let's find somewhere to stay before everywhere's booked up.'

Luckily they got rooms in the Cruachan Hotel with spectacular views across Loch Linnhe to the Morvern Hills. But Beth barely glanced at the scenery. She was here for a reason, a reason that might change her life forever.

Once they'd unpacked their meagre luggage and freshened up, they enjoyed a coffee in the bar. Her throat was dry and she ordered a second cup. 'What now?' she asked.

'We could go to the library, look up old newspapers. Maybe get a better insight.'

She nodded, still unsure, glad he was with her.

James briefly explained to the librarian what they were looking for.

'The Oban Times or the Press and Journal would be your best bet,' she said. 'Unfortunately you can only access The Press and Journal on-line. We do have back copies of the Oban Times, however.' She took them to the archives. 'The years are printed on the shelves.' She ran her fingers lightly across the spines. 'You say you know the date? Then it shouldn't be hard to find.' She pulled out around five newspapers. 'The article you're looking for should definitely be in one of those. If you want access to the computer give me a shout.'

James handed two papers to Beth. 'You look in these, I'll start the others.'

Within five minutes, he smacked his hand on an open page. 'I've found it.'

Beth's breath stopped. She rose and leaned over his shoulder. The headline, black and severe, screamed back at her.

Body found beneath the Low Falls.

Yesterday the body of a boy was pulled from beneath the Lower Falls in Glen Nevis. Identity has not yet been verified, but the search for twelve-year-old Michael MacLean has been called off. Michael and his sister, Elizabeth, had been taken on a picnic by their mother, Veronica MacLean, aged thirty-one. At one stage, Veronica fell asleep in the sun. When she woke up both children were missing.

After she read it, Beth sat down, her legs suddenly weak, her blood hot. For a long time she stared at her hands.

'You're very quiet,' said James, after a moment.

'My poor mother,' she whispered. 'She must have blamed herself, and possibly my father blamed her too. I guess that's why she went away.'

'It could well have been.'

'My mother left and my father was barely interested.' Beth suddenly felt a rush of anger. 'I was only a little girl and I thought everything was my fault.'

He put his arm around her. 'Now you know the truth, it will get easier.'

She lifted tear-stained eyes to his. 'It was so hard, reading that. I need a drink.' The cold which crept over her as she stood before the cottage reclaimed her and she shuddered.

'All right?' asked James.

'Someone walked over my grave.' She tightened her scarf around her neck.

He took her arm, led her back to the car and drove to the hotel. Except for one old man sitting at the bar, the room was empty. They found a seat in a cosy corner beside wall-high book-shelves and a realistic gas fire in a stone wall. He bought a brandy and a glass of coke and set the brandy in front of Beth.

She reached for the glass with a shaking hand. In her head she could hear Andy ranting. *'You shouldn't have done this. Now you've opened another can of worms. This could bring back the nightmares, give you a relapse.'*

'Hah, Andy,' she answered mentally, 'The nightmares never truly left me.'

James placed his hand over hers and the warmth gave her courage to take a step back in her mind. The past leaked in too quickly and she was back in that day, the sun hot against her skin, with only a gentle breeze to lift her curls.

'No Michael, Dad'll be mad.'

'He won't know.' He turned and his face was inches from hers. And she saw him clearly. Dark hair, blue eyes, a handsome boy. 'You won't tell him, will you?'

She swallowed the brandy, closing her eyes against the burn in her throat.

'You've remembered something, haven't you?' asked James.

Beth nodded. She took a breath. 'I was happy. We didn't go near the falls, but ate the picnic beside the burn. I was picking daisies. My mother was stringing them together and she was singing something. Michael was... '

She could see him behind her closed eyelids. He was pretending to fight something or someone with a stick for a sword, jumping about, slashing the air.

101

The day had been warm, the hum of bees, the scent of heather, the tinkle of water over stone, her mother's soft lovely voice. Michael shouting at his unseen enemy.

'It was such a lovely day,' Beth said. 'That's all I remember.' She didn't want to talk about it, didn't want to explain.

James squeezed the hand in his. 'Just relax. Don't try to force it or block it. I'll get you another brandy.'

'Put some lemonade in it this time,' she said.

Her mother fell asleep, the article said. When had that happened?

'Enough,' she whispered to her subconscious, 'I've had enough for one day.'

'What did you say?' James set the drinks on the table.

'Nothing, just thinking aloud.' She grabbed the drink and threw it back.

'You're shaking.' James looked concerned. 'Take it slowly.'

She set the empty glass on the table and hung her head, closing her eyes. 'I'm beginning to remember and I don't want to.'

'It may get worse, but then it will get better. Trust me, I'll be here beside you every step of the way.'

She turned to him. 'Do you mind if I go to my room? I feel exhausted.' She stood up, longing to be alone with her thoughts.

'But we haven't eaten,' he said. 'Let's order something first.'

'Go ahead without me, I couldn't eat.'

'If you need me, give me a call.'

'Sure thing,' she said to the floor.

102

Back in her room, she lay on her bed and stared at the ceiling. 'Just relax,' James had said. The brandy already dulled her senses and she allowed herself to drift away as she faced the images filling her head.

Her mother was asleep, snoring gently. She had been drinking from a bottle which smelled funny and now lay empty by her side.

'Look, an eagle,' shouted Michael, and Beth's eyes followed his pointing finger. The eagle hung in the sky, far above them, circling slowly.

'Quick, hide,' yelled Michael, grabbing her arm and dragging her behind a gorse bush.

Her heart beat frantically. 'Why?' she asked, his urgency terrifying her.

He lowered his voice to a whisper. 'Me and Ian Magee climbed way up there last week, right up to the eagle's nest and then we broke all the eggs. Now the eagle is looking for us. She'll kill us for sure when she catches us. You too, because you're with me.'

Beth believed him. At four years old she believed everything her brother told her. She glanced towards the sky and imagined the eagle was drawing ever closer.

'They hunt you down,' he continued. 'They never stop until they've found you and ripped your guts out.'

Beth started to cry.

'We'll have to kill her, hunt her down first. Come on.'

Beth shook her head. 'I'm not going.'

'Then stay here, but hide.'

She looked at her mother, still snoring. 'Don't go away,' she pleaded.

'Then come too, but stay low.'

'Tell Mam. Mam, Mam ...' Her mother didn't move.

'You know how she gets. She won't waken.'

'But the eagle will get her.'

'Then we'll kill it first.'

He ran towards the falls. She ran after him, as fast as her short legs could carry her, constantly looking up at the sky. The eagle still circled ever lower, watching her.

'Come on. It's an adventure. I know what to do.' Then Michael took her hand, something he never did in front of people. 'Quickly now. I'm Dan Dare and you're the princess. I'm rescuing you from the evil witch.'

'What about the eagle?'

'He's the evil witch's pet.'

'Who's the evil witch?'

'Aunt Moira. She only pretends to be kind. She's really fattening us up so she can eat us. See how she always gives us sweeties?'

Beth nodded. She liked Aunt Moira. The kind lady who made tablet toffee which she shared with the children.

'I don't want to play this.'

'Don't be such a baby. Come on.'

Michael was always calling her a baby. She hated it. She wanted to be all grown up like him and not afraid of anything.

And then the eagle landed on a ledge above the Lower Falls. It wasn't a dignified landing, or even, it appeared to her now, a decision made by the bird. More of a weakening of the wings, a hopeless beating against the inevitable, a desperate opening and shutting of the beak. Now, through adult eyes, she realised the bird had been hurt, dying, but as a young child, she saw it as a predator come to destroy her and her brother.

'Wow, look at that,' Michael breathed. 'We can get him now.'

They ran towards the Falls, across the bridge and up the other side until her legs were tired and yet he kept going forward, dragging her behind. 'Stop crying,' he shouted. She was afraid of Michael when he shouted.

'I want to go home,' she whimpered.

'We can't go home yet. We've got to kill the eagle.'

'We shouldn't kill birds. Mam says.'

'What does Mam know? He's going to kill us.' Then he stopped and pointed upward. 'He's looking at us, get down.' He dragged her down with him into the heather. The roughness scratched her face. Her heart thumped.

'Don't worry,' said Michael. 'I'll protect you.' He sprang to his feet. Then he stopped, his voice suddenly losing all excitement. 'It's hurt. We need to help it. If we save it, maybe we can keep it, teach it not to be wicked.'

Michael was all seriousness now. 'He might become our friend, give us rides on his back and stuff.'

'I want Mam.'

'You won't tell we came up here,' he said, rounding on her.

'Don't kill the eagle, please.'

He laughed at her. 'You're so silly. I wouldn't kill an eagle. Honestly, you'd believe anything. Stay here. I'm going to climb over, see what's wrong with it.'

105

And she looked at the eagle across from them now. It lifted its head and saw her, but its eyes were dull, empty, and even then, she knew life was leaking from it. Her fear became greater, as if somehow she had been responsible. She cried louder then, not only from fear, but also from sorrow.

She watched Michael clamber down into the gulf and up the other side towards the bird. The bird that now lay still, it's eyes open, already looking inward, towards some other place.

Michael hoisted himself onto the ledge beside the eagle. Turning his head to look at Beth, he screeched, 'I think it's dead.'

Beth watched as the head lifted. She saw the beak open. The wing rose. She parted her lips to shout a warning. Her breath was hot against her tongue. The wing fell, its feathers brushing Michael. Her voice came from her heart and broke the air.

Michael turned his head to look at her. At the same instant that her brother heard her warning, the bird slashed at him with its beak. Beth did not know, could not see, whether the wing knocked him, or he stepped backwards to escape. Michael's head twisted back towards the eagle, but his body kept moving. One foot lifted and fought for purchase, the earth slipped away and he was falling, over the edge of the precipice, tumbling, bouncing from rock to rock, down the sides of the waterfall. And the rushing of the water and the sound of his scream fragmented the air around her.

She watched him fall. She saw the blood on his face and hands. She heard the splash as he hit the water and

106

disappeared below. The eagle lay still. The mountain rose sharply. Rolling banks of mist stretched fingers towards her, down the hillside. Then there were no more screams, only the thunder of the water. A black shadow filled the sky above her. Without any idea of where she was, she opened her mouth to cry for her mother, but only a pathetic mewling came out. There the memory faded, leaving her shaken to the core.

After an age of staring into the darkness, her heart beating hard against her ribcage, she rose from the bed and wrapped her dressing gown around her. The shaking had taken over her body and she needed a drink, needed company. She went out into the corridor and to James' door. Stopping for no longer than a heartbeat, she lifted her hand and knocked.

A sleepy-eyed James opened the door. 'Beth...' She pushed past him and into the room.

'I remember,' she said. 'I remember it all. I thought it was my fault. I didn't shout in time. I saw the eagle move and my voice froze. I can't... I can't be alone tonight.'

He opened his arms and she fell into them. He led her to the bed and set her down.

I remembered,' she said. 'Not leaving Fort William or coming to Berriedale, but what happened on the mountain.' She took a deep breath and told him everything in a monotone. When she finished she leaned against him, drawing on his strength, then she turned and rested her head on his shoulder as he held her, stroking her back and making soothing noises.

'It was dreadful, terrible. I think I'd rather not know.'

'You can move on from here,' he whispered. 'I promise.'

'If I shouted sooner, warned him...'

'If he hadn't climbed up to where the bird was, if your mother hadn't fallen asleep, if you had not gone on a picnic. Life is full of ifs and buts.'

'But I saw the bird move. It wasn't dead.'

'You were children, both of you.'

She drew back and looked into his face. 'It wasn't my fault, was it?'

'Of course it wasn't.'

'I think... I think my mother had a drink problem. Why else would she take her children on a picnic and then drink herself into a stupor? I can see her now, drinking from the bottle, her speech starting to get slurred, then telling us to go and play while she took a wee nap.'

'Sounds logical.'

'I want to go to his grave.'

'Of course.'

'Tomorrow.'

'Yes, tomorrow.'

'Come on then, let's try and get some sleep.' He pulled back the duvet. She crawled under it. 'Lie beside me,' she whispered. 'Just hold me. I need to be held. Nothing else.'

'That was my only intention.' He crawled in beside her.

Chapter Twelve

At six o'clock in the morning, Beth was wakened by the sharp melody of her ringtone. For a moment she couldn't imagine where she was. Her head felt thick. Within the time it took to reach across and grab her mobile, memory flooded in. Beside her, James stirred and scratched his head. He rolled towards her and put an arm around her waist.

'Yes, thanks, I'll come right away.' She slammed the phone on the bedside table and threw the duvet off.

'What was that?' said James, half sitting, his eyes still heavy with sleep.

'Raigmore Hospital. My father. He's... he's...' She took a deep breath and stopped.

James pulled himself out of bed and stood beside her. 'Is he...?'

'He's speaking. He's agitated and desperate to see me.' Her voice shook. 'We have to go back, *now*.'

'Yes, yes of course.'

Beth suddenly realised James was wearing only a pair of loose shorts.

Embarrassed, she pulled her eyes away, grabbed her dressing gown and struggled into it, speed making her clumsy. 'Meet you downstairs, in ten minutes.' She fisted her mussed up hair and fled from his room.

Two hours later, Beth sat by her father's side holding his hand. When he opened his eyes, they filled with recognition. Bloodless lips moved but no sound came out.

'It's all right, Dad, I'm here,' she said.

His eyes filled with tears. The lips parted again. 'Be Be...Be..,Bethy,' the word was forced from him, until finally he lay back exhausted.

'Yes, It's Beth.'

'I....,' his body tensed, he struggled to say more.

'It's all right.'

His body tensed again. 'Mi ... Mi ... Mi ...'

'Michael. Dad, I know about Michael, and I understand so much more.'

Questions filled his eyes.

'It must have been so hard for you.' She felt her own tears threaten. Please God, she prayed silently, give me enough time with him to mend this relationship.

He still seemed agitated. 'Le... tt... er. I mean...meant, you ...'

She bent her ear close to his mouth. 'You meant to write me, is that what you're saying? It's okay. I understand now. I understand about the depression.'

'No... no. Ver... your mam, for you... letter.' His agitation grew. His voice was so low and slurred she could hardly make out the words.

'My mam? Are you saying my mam wrote me a letter?' For a moment the old anger filled her again. Had her mother written to her, had he kept that letter from her?

'I didn't know... You gone. I wrote to... the address.... No reply. Never... any... reply.' His sank back into his pillow.

110

'You wrote to the address I gave you?'

A slight nod.

'I got no letter.' A coldness filled her up. *Andy.* If she harboured any doubts about cutting him out of her life, they vanished at that moment.

'Did you send my mother's letter there?'

He shook his head. Relief flooded her. 'Where's the letter now?'

'It's... all I had... of... her. Took... her with... me.'

He lifted his hand as if indicating the locker.

Beth pulled open the doors and removed the contents. Only his toiletries, a spare pair of pyjamas, a pair of slippers. On the bottom shelf was a pair of trousers, vest, socks and a shirt, folded neatly. She felt in the trouser pockets. Nothing there.

Robbie's breathing was coming fast now, his lips faintly blue.

Beth went to the door of the room and called. 'Nurse.'

Within seconds a young nurse hurried into the room and picked up Robbie's wrist.

'Was there a letter? He says he had a letter.'

Her face brightened. 'Yes, he did have a letter in his trouser pocket. We kept it, although, you understand, he'd been lying alone for quite a while. We had to wash his clothes.' She looked apologetic. 'I'll ask the charge nurse where she put the letter.'

A few minutes later she returned and handed Beth a crumpled unopened envelope, torn at the corners.

'Seems like he's been carrying it around,' the nurse said. 'Must mean a lot to him.'

111

Beth sat down again. She wouldn't read it now. She wanted to be alone, in her own home, have time to digest the words. Only then, if she thought it appropriate, would she read it to her father.

'I've got it now,' she whispered. The old man relaxed. A faint lop-sided smile played around his mouth.

'I'm going to get the cottage renovated, made fit for a disabled person, then you'll come home and live with me.'

He opened his eyes. his head moved slowly from side to side. 'No. Your... life.'

'Yes, my life to make my own decisions. And I'm staying.' The smile rose unbidden from her heart and stretched her cheeks.

She spent another hour by his bedside, telling him some of her past, about her poems and how she'd been publishing them under a pseudonym, about James and how they found out about Michael, how she intended to lay flowers on his grave. She barely mentioned Andy.

The tautness of his cheeks relaxed. Without sound, his lips formed the words, 'Thank you.'

As James drove her home that night, she told him about the letter from her mother, and about the letters she never received. Afterwards, she felt more positive than ever before.

'We can go back as soon as you like. I'm doing nothing else anyway.'

'Could you stay for a little while when you drop me off?' Beth asked. 'I need company.'

The car crested the top of the hill and she could see across the glen to her cottage on the opposite brae. The low sun caught the window-panes turning them to fire, and glinted on something else sitting a short distance from the door. With a collapsing of spirit, she recognised Andy's car.

'My God, it's Andy,' she said. 'I have to do this myself. James, could you go home and let me use your car? I'll bring it back when he's gone.'

'Are you sure? I could come with you.'

'No, I'm sure.'

James drove up his own drive and handed the keys to her. 'Later then?' he said.

'Later.' She climbed into the driver's seat, her mouth dry, and turned the key in the ignition with a trembling hand.

Driving slowly, she negotiated the bend and the narrow road which led to the cottage.

Andy stood still, as if carved from stone, watching as her car drew up, one hand in his pocket. From the other his keys dangled.

She knew she had to face him, but she had no wish to do so at this moment. She needed time to think, to prepare.

'Andy,' she said as she exited her car. 'I was going to call you.' She swallowed, her throat dry.

He moved one hand, jingling the keys. He tossed them up and caught them as they fell. His fingers closed over them. She heard his intake of breath.

'Not before time,' he said. 'Well, have you got this stupidity out of your system?'

113

Trying to avoid body contact, she edged past him and opened the door. 'I found out what I wanted to know, if that's what you mean.'

He followed her into the house. 'And what has it proved?'

'Aren't you even interested?'

'Of course I'm interested. You can tell me all about it on the way home.'

After setting her bag on the table, she turned to look into his face. 'I want my share of the business. I need the money.'

His jaw dropped. 'What? What's brought this on? It's that... that James isn't it?' The chill from his eyes made the cold room even colder. 'I should have made you come home sooner.'

Beth laughed an unhappy laugh. 'You. Should. Have. Made me? That's been the problem. You always tell me what to do, what to think. My father wrote to me didn't he? When I was a mess.'

Andy's expression froze.

'What happened to the letters, Andy?'

For the first time he faltered, his face reddened. 'What letters? No, he didn't.'

But she knew he was lying. She knew by the slight change in the tone of his voice, by the way his eyes became wary, by the angle of his head. It suddenly occurred to her he had lied a lot to her over the years.

'Yes. I destroyed them.' He regained his composure. 'You were so vulnerable. The letters would have only done you harm. It was to protect you. Everything I've ever done was to protect you. But it was never good enough, was it?' He turned away, an injured look on his face.

'I'll always be grateful you took me back after London. But you never let me forget it. And you didn't want me to remember. Didn't want me to have any other life before you.'

'What are you on about? I was the one who put you into therapy.'

'Yes, and the one who took me out when I reached the most crucial point. You made me feel worthless. You kept those letters because you didn't want anyone else in my life, even my own parents.'

His eyes rounded. His lips moved. He caught himself. She noted his stance, the way he narrowed his eyes and, as he opened his mouth to speak, she held up her hand. 'Don't bother to lie to me.'

He turned his gaze from her and instead studied the window and the gathering night beyond it. 'You were a mess. For God's sake, what good would the letters have done? Just upset you all over again. You were just beginning to get yourself together.'

'You convinced me any doubts I had about you were all in my mind. Just like my inability to sing. I blamed myself. I was useless – you made me feel useless. I know I made bad choices, and I've paid, I've paid so much. I cared about you, but I'm not in love with you.'

'Fuck's sake! I gave you everything.'

'Everything except the truth! No one knew what it was like for me, not even you. I always had a face for the public.'

115

'You had the club, your poetry, and a damn fine standard of living. I thought you were happy the way things were.'

'Did you ever stop to ask? I always walked one step ahead of this black dog that followed me. I needed to turn and face it and every time I tried, you turned me back again. And guess what?' She laughed again. 'It's not so bad. I can deal with it now. And, Andy, however many years I have left, I don't want to spend them with you.'

His face changed. Shock, horror, anger. She saw them all flit through his eyes, and then, finally, panic.

'I won't make it without you,' he said, suddenly contrite. 'You're my whole life.'

'You'll make it with Glenda. Yes, I've seen the way she looks at you, and you're not totally opposed to her attention. It was my money that bought the club, but I only want half. There'll be enough for you to set up someplace smaller.'

'Glenda, wh... at? It's you I want. We'll fire Glenda if she's the problem.'

'She's nothing. Definitely not the problem.' Beth was sure of herself now.

'Is this all about the letters? You were off your head, I couldn't risk giving them to you. You have no idea what you put me through.' His fists clenched.

'There you go again, making it all my fault.'

She heard the air hiss though his teeth, saw the anger in his eyes.

'If you don't come home now, tonight, don't bother calling me from a mental hospital begging for my help.

116

It's over, hear me, over. And don't expect a penny from the business.'

'If that's how it must be, I'll see you in court.'

He stared at her. His lips parted. The colour in his face intensified. She thought he was going to say more. Then he abruptly snapped his mouth closed, turned on his heel and marched out slamming the door hard.

Trembling, Beth sank into a chair and resisted the urge to reach for the wine bottle. Shadows of the night grew longer and dusk crept into the corners. The warm body of the cat pressed itself against her legs as if sensing her need for comfort. She rose, switched on the light, returned to the couch and picked up the cat. He immediately nestled on her knee and began to purr. Without disturbing the animal, she reached for her handbag and withdrew the letter. Her hand shook as she prised the flap open. She held onto it for a long moment seeing only the neat, slanting handwriting, feeling the smooth cream paper, the small roses along the top. It looked like the kind of paper which would have been scented once. She lifted it to her nose, but any fragrance had long gone. Finally, she found the strength to read the words.

My darling Bethy,

Today you will be 21 years old. I hope your father has arranged a lovely party for you. I've wanted to write to you for so long. The one time I tried to see you, I was told you were happy, and I was afraid, afraid to disrupt your life. Now you are all grown up, I hope you will understand my reasons for leaving and forgive me. I was wrong I know, I should have taken you with me, but I was such a mess at the time. It was my fault your brother died, I couldn't risk harming you too. I went to Edinburgh and then to London, but I couldn't settle. If I couldn't have you, then I had to be near Michael. I'm going to move back to Fort William where I can visit his grave. As soon as I find a place to stay, maybe you'll come and see me?

My love forever
Mam.
P.S. If you want to make contact, here is my number.

Then followed an old number, which Beth knew would be obsolete since the area codes had changed many years ago. She couldn't have read it anyway. By this time her eyes were blurry. Still clutching the letter, she dried her cheeks. 'Oh, Mam,' she whispered. 'If only I'd known. Damn Andy. Damn him to hell.' All this time, her mother had been in Fort William, just across the country. Years after she'd written this letter, she would have read all about Beth, everything in the papers. Maybe she bought her records, maybe she'd even been at one of her shows, maybe she'd been in the crowd waiting by the stage door – hell, she might have even given her an autograph.

Needing to speak to someone, needing to hear words of reassurance, Beth walked outside, letter in hand, and drove to James' house.

As soon as he answered the door, she grabbed his hand. 'I'm so glad to see you,' she whispered. 'My relationship with Andy is over.'

'You're sure?'

'If I wasn't before, I am now. If only I had known about the letters, my life could have been so different. I thought Andy was my saviour, but really, he took so much from me. I could never forgive him for that.' She dropped his hand and went to turn away. 'He wanted my voice, my contacts, my money, my expertise.' Her tone became bitter. 'He wants to own me, but I doubt if he ever loved me. Make me a cup of coffee –and make it strong, no scrub that, give me a drink.'

'Leave it for now.' He grabbed her arm, pulled her towards him and gently cupped her face in his hand. She steeled herself and met his eyes. The wind rose outside, the trees scraped the windowpane, a shower of determined sleet suddenly rattled the glass, but she felt warm and safe. Beth held the eye contact, allowing him to gaze into her face, aware of the crow's feet around her eyes, the lines running down either side of her mouth, the loose skin around her jaw-line.

'I've earned every one of them,' she said.

'What?'

'The lines.' She smiled.

'What lines?' Half closing his eyes, he bent his head until his lips brushed hers. The merest touch, yet enough to let her know irrevocably, why she had never agreed to marry Andy. And suddenly, as his arms tightened around her, a song rose in her heart, and she knew at that moment she *would* sing again.

Chapter Thirteen

Walking up the drive of the neat cottage on the outskirts of Fort William, her head lowered, James' hand in hers, Beth ignored the slanting sleet. This time the door was open by a woman about Beth's own age, plump and warm with a face that spoke of contentment.

'Sorry to bother you, but I wondered... well, I was born in this house,' said Beth.

The woman's eyes opened wide. She gave a little gasp and stepped back. 'Come on in, my deary. My name's Maggie by the way.'

Beth followed her into a bright living room, explaining who she was as she went, her words as quick as her footsteps.

Maggie turned to the couple. 'I know who you are. Veronica is my aunt. So we're cousins. Take a seat till I get a cuppa and then we'll talk.' She raised her eyebrows, 'Tea, coffee?'

Her cousin? Beth couldn't sit. Instead she walked around the room, looking at photos, wondering who the smiling faces were. Her relations? She never knew she had an aunt, cousins. Aunt Moira? The name sprang into her mind. Aunt Moira who made them tablet toffee. She ran her finger over a stack of LPs stored sideways in the unit. She edged one out. With a gasp, she found herself looking at a picture of her twenty-six-year old self, her red hair floating in a manufactured breeze, her dress blown back, her perfect figure shown to full advantage as the material clung to the curves of her body, so provocative for the era. It was one of the only two LPs she'd ever produced.

'Veronica bought them,' said Maggie, coming back into the room carrying a tray which she set on the pine coffee table.

Beth took a seat. She didn't add milk to her tea. Her hand was shaking too much.

'She spoke a lot about her little girl, her beautiful little girl,' Maggie said. 'We all thought you weren't interested. She was so proud when you became well-known. We encouraged her to get in touch, but she said it was up to you. She didn't want you to think she was after a handout.'

'What... what happened to her, my mother?'

Maggie set her cup to one side. 'What do you remember of her?'

'I remember thinking she was a beautiful queen.' Beth allowed her mind to drift back. 'And she sang as she did stuff. She and my father shouted at each other a lot and she often cried.' Then a more disturbing memory pushed itself in. 'Sometimes she would speak funny and fall asleep. I... we... couldn't wake her. I got so I could recognise the smell of Mammy's illness.' She raised her eyes to her cousin's. 'I know now it was alcohol. Was she a drunk?'

'I was young, too. But I did hear she liked a drink.'

'She was drunk the day she took Michael and me up the glen. Why else would she have fallen asleep?'

'I don't know about then. Later, after she came back here, she never touched a drop.'

121

Beth leaned forward. 'She sent me a letter. I never received it until a few days ago.'

'Is that why you didn't get in touch?' Maggie shook her head. 'What wasted years. She didn't expect you to reply, but it hurt her nonetheless.'

'Is she buried locally? Beside Michael?' asked James.

'Oh, no, love, Veronica isn't dead.'

Beth's stomach roiled.

'She has a pensioner's flat in town. She manages well, despite her age.'

'Where... where is she?' Beth's chest tightened. Outside the rain had stopped and a shaft of sunlight brightened the room.

Maggie glanced at the clock on the mantle. 'About now, she'll be visiting your brother.'

Beth spun around. Her eyes trapped James'. 'The graveyard,' she breathed, then, turning to Maggie, she reached towards her. 'Thank you, thank you so much.'

They stopped at the supermarket and bought the largest bunch of flowers on sale. The cemetery was easily found, and Maggie's directions to the grave easily followed.

The ground still glistened after the last shower. The sun cast beams through a break in the overcast sky. From somewhere a curlew gave a lonely hoot. Apart from the two of them, the cemetery was empty of human life.

'Maybe she's a bit late,' said James closing his fingers gently on Beth's arm.

'Yes. Maybe.' She looked around once more and moistened her lips, disappointed. Beth laid the flowers on the slight mound and ran her hand over the marble of the gravestone. She traced the lettering with her finger.

In Loving Memory of
Michael Robert MacLean
Darling son of Robert and Veronica MacLean.
Brother of Elizabeth
2/10/43 - 29/9/55
Safe in the arms of Jesus

Silently she stood up, eyes still on the words.
'I wish I'd known him better.' She shivered. The chill of winter was already in the air, the higher of the Munros already white-capped. A poem about this day was forming in her head, a poem in which Michael spoke, using her as his channel.

'Come on,' said James gently. 'We'll go find your mother.' Together they turned around and stopped. There, coming towards them were two people, one young, pushing a wheelchair, the other in the wheelchair, elderly, a tartan rug wrapped around her legs, a bunch of flowers in her lap.

For a moment Beth froze, unable to speak and a rush of blood filled her up as both women gazed at each other. The old woman gave a little cry and extended her arms.

The sun found another break in the clouds and turned the mountain-tops to fire. Above them an eagle circled and rode the thermals.

Epilogue

Robbie

The clock strikes midnight and I wait for him to return, and as I wait the light gathers and becomes intense. I embrace it. I am ready.

I have watched my younger child grow from a baby into a bright, happy toddler. Her smile lit up my morning, her chuckles lifted the darkest cloud. But after it happened, the thing that destroyed my family, she became a shadow. And the shadow writhed within a greater shadow cast by her parent's pain and blaming of each other.

We returned to Berriedale at the onset of winter and we took our black cloud with us. When Veronica went, she left an even darker cloud in its place.

The child cowered and shivered and railed and became a wild cat, striking out at the world. So great was my pain, I was unable to reach hers. I watched her grow, afraid to love too much, knowing one day I would lose her too.

She went before I was ready to let go. She went and took with her my final reason for life. I searched for her in the streets of London, as I had not searched for her mother. I spent long nights walking the pavements, showing her photo to anyone who would look and grew accustomed to the shaking of heads. Police, Salvation Army, the destitute and hopeless who slept in shop doorways, beneath bridges, in cardboard cities.

124

Finally, I went home and took up such as was left of my existence, my concern and guilt a living snake that twisted in my heart. Then the letter came to say she was well and happy. No address, Edinburgh postmark. Had she been there all along?

Even then, I believed she would come back when she was ready.

Suddenly her picture was everywhere. She had become a sensation. A singer. The new voice on the London scene. Had I really imagined that she would need me? Perhaps she never had.

Then one day she did get in touch with an address. She was back in Edinburgh. I lifted a hesitant pen and scrawled out words of joy. The following week I wrote another, pleading with her to keep in touch. Seven times I sent similar words, my world collapsing a little bit more with every passing day, with every empty post.

I thought I understood her reasons for ignoring my letters. I could see her in my mind's eye, like the pictures on the cover of her LPs, her hair long and as it had been as a child, still the same shade of reddish gold as my own, her body willowy, like her mother.

One night, perhaps, having drunk too much and in a fit of nostalgia, she would have written to me, regretting it upon waking the next day. Perhaps she had no memory of having put pen to paper at all. My final letter told her that on her twenty-first birthday, I'd received word from her mother. I should have told her sooner, but now I felt sure it would bring a response. When I was still met by silence, I knew it was over. She would not come back.

As I lay in my hospital bed, no one knowing I was still inside my shell, still able to think, to rationalise, to pray, I saw him in the sun-rays from the window, shimmering, smiling at me, and I knew him. Michael. He held out his hands. He had come to take me to that other place. I rose from my body reluctantly and pleaded with him to leave me until Beth came back to me, until she forgave me, until she knew about him, her brother. I told him I had more to do. He nodded and he shrunk and his light diminished and the window swung open.

She did come, asked for my forgiveness. And I couldn't leave my shell to tell her what was in my heart. My mouth was full of words but my lips and teeth and tongue could not make them whole.

Today she returned. She has found Veronica. She has found the place where Michael's bones rest. She has found peace. She tells me she'll see me tomorrow. I mouth, 'I love you.' She drops a kiss on my forehead. We communicate now without words.

The clock strikes midnight and I wait for him to return, and as I wait the light gathers and becomes intense. Behind him are two other shapes, shadows gradually becoming whole. I recognise my parents. This time I'm ready. Beth will see me in her dreams, she will see me and Michael standing together, happy and healthy, and she will wake and know I have gone.

I discard my useless body and float towards the outstretched arms. The silver thread that binds me to this earth snaps and I am free.

126

Other books by this author

Follow the Dove

The Broken Horizon

The Road to Nowhere.

***

Gone With the Tide and other Stories.

www.Catherinebyrne-author.com

Printed in Great Britain
by Amazon

33297805R00076